Wild and Penned

by

the Grosmont Writers' Group

GWG

www.antonywootten.co.uk

GWG is an imprint of
Eskdale Publishing, UK

First published in Great Britain in 2016 by
Eskdale Publishing, North Yorkshire

A Catalogue record for this book is available from the British
Library.

ISBN: 978-0-9935042-2-8

Printed and bound in the UK by
York Publishing Services
www.yps-publishing.co.uk

Grosmont Writers' Group: 3 years on!

This book is the Grosmont Writers' Group's second anthology. The first one, Time Well Spent, was such a success we thought we'd give it another go.

As a writers' group, we have been meeting fortnightly for more than four years now. In our meetings we take it in turns to read something we've written − a chapter, a poem, a story − and the group provides suggestions and constructive criticism. It may sound arduous, but friendship, joviality and a mutual commitment to producing our best work make it a thoroughly pleasurable process.

The scrutiny often extends to Paula's homebrew and Delphine's cakes, which are all as close to perfection as it's humanly possible to achieve. If our writing comes anywhere near rivalling their quality, we are doing pretty well.

And I think it does. I hope you will agree when you read this book. Like our first, it is filled with a variety of tales from wild imaginations, penned through pain and passion for your reading pleasure.

Antony Wootten

Contents

Baby Tim's Tale

Paula Harrison

I'm allus called 'Baby Tim'. I think I'll be 'Baby Tim' forever, it's one of them names that you get stuck with.

There's three generations of us lot on our farm. I love it. I was born on a stormy night ten years ago. Rain was coming down sideways and Dad had to ride down to t'village on Sparky for t'midwife.

I get a lot of attention from everyone, all eager to teach me farming skills. I listen and enjoy learning. I'd rather be at home than stuck at school. Mam says I need an education as t'world will change in my lifetime. My education is t'farm as that's what I want to do.

Grandad and Dad show me how to harness t'Shire horses and care for 'em. We work hard. I have my little jobs: I feed orphan lambs. I wish there were lambs all year round; I think sheep are ugly when they grow up. I have a dozen ducks and hens to care for as well. Dad says I can sell t'eggs and keep t'money. I've got a few bob put by. I have me own garden plot where I grow taties, a few tonnups, carrots and lettuce. Our farm's high up and we get t'easterly winds. Me dad says that's why all that we can grow up 'ere is root crops.

I like helping wi' t'logging, but Dad says I'm not

1

big enough nor old enough to use t'big axe yet. Anyway, there's a dead tree blown down and we need to collect it. Mam says t'range eats wood so we best be quick.

Grandad built a set of football goal posts in the corner of t'lower field. All t'kids in t'village come up and we have some 'appy times. Grandad sometimes comes to referee. You don't argue as he was captain of t'village team for twenty years.

I got a clip round me ear'ole from me mam t'other day. Nana asked if I wanted to learn how to mek bread, I told her it was women's work and wanted to be outside not stuck in't kitchen with a load of women.

On Sundays we go to church. Most of my class are in t'choir. We hid t'matches last week so t'choir master couldn't light t'oil lamp. But then Alan went and gave t'game away by laughing.

I like visiting me mates on other farms. Our David lends me his bike but I prefer riding Sparky, although I am not quite big enough for him yet. But Sparky's sensible and I know I am safe on him. Anyway, I still have to be home before it gets dark. We play in buildings and stack yards, we dam up rivers and catch fish.

In t'winter we build snowmen and chuck snowballs. Last time it snowed I got another clip round me ear, this one off me dad. He was leading t'awd bull and I chucked a snowball at him. It were right on target so I reckon it was worth it.

Grandad made me a sledge out of an old box.

It's fastest of t'lot. We have races down t'field. There's a couple of bends and we have to get through t'gate at t'bottom, otherwise we're straight into t'stone wall, and that hurts. When I get in I'm usually soaked and Nana dries all me clothes round t'range.

Nana never lets me draw t'fire using newspaper, she says it's dangerous. The other day I'd set off for school and realised I'd left me book in't kitchen. Nana was in on her own and she was drawing t'fire with newspaper. She was surprised and embarrassed to see me back. She called t'fire a rude word and said she needed t'oven hot and some hot water and t'fire wouldn't go. She told me not to tell me mam. I won't say owt 'coz Nana's good to us all.

I can't wait for Christmas. Everybody seems to come round and see us at Christmas. We eat in t'kitchen, then we all move into t'front room and sit round t'fire. It's not very often that we're allowed in there. Nana and Mam dish out port, ginger wine, beer, and owt else that anyone wants; homemade lemonade for me 'coz they say I'm not old enough for t'ard stuff. Not only are we in t'front room, but those glasses with pheasants on 'em come out; we only see them at Christmas!

At New Year we all go to Uncle Bill's farm. It's a chance to catch up with all me cousins. We stay up until midnight and then kiss everyone. Yuk! Me dad got drunk last year and got a right earful from me mam. I don't think he'll do that again.

It's 1939 next year. I heard Mam and our Janet talking. They said there was a big cloud over Europe. I hope that means it'll snow all winter so we can get t'sledge out again.

The strange affair of Septimus Black

Paul Wootten

He had been hanging around for some time, watching her as she sat by the bar, her big eyes fixed on a youth who didn't seem to have noticed her. She smiled as the barman served a drink. Her legs swung teasingly as she sat there.

'If only she would look at me like that', he thought. She slid smoothly from the stool, slunk over to the young guy and seemed to whisper something to him, then the two of them left the bar together. Jealousy surged up inside him. There was no way that that youngster could satisfy her, he thought. Why had she not looked at him?

Business kept him from the bar for several days, and when next he stood quietly there sipping some nameless, warm brown liquid, she walked in alone and took up her usual place. The barman served another a drink. Would she notice him there in the dark corner? He watched her, tantalized by her beauty, the hour-glass shape of her delicious body and her gorgeous eyes. How wonderful it would be if he could find some reason to approach her. In his mind he explored situations where they might meet, and fantasized about them: he might find himself walking beside her in the hotel garden, watching the flies play around the flower-heads; he could, by chance, share the hotel lift with her. He realized that he had been lost in dreams, for when he looked again he was shocked to see that she was staring straight at him. Those wide eyes fixing him like snares and pulling him to her. Without thought, he rose and walked towards her. He could smell the delicious perfume as she bent over him. She touched him gently and a shiver of delight tingled its way through him. She beckoned and he followed.

Transported on a web of thrilling expectation he fumbled his way along as eventually she led the way into her chamber. She was good. Oh, she was very good. Before he knew it she was lying beside him on the soft bed of gossamer; her silk sheets, white as snow and filled with the delicious aroma of musk, slipped over him. Nothing, he thought, could be as good as this! She caressed him and encouraged him to explore her beauty. Each time he turned to her she was watching him with those big eyes. She smiled encouragement, her broad mouth enticing with every movement. Rhythmically they performed together. He was intrigued by her strength, as he thrust she held his shoulders in a grip of steel. In one sudden moment of ecstasy he gave her everything.

Sweat stood out on his face as he pulled himself

away. She rolled over on top of him. He saw her big eyes and her gorgeous mouth, slightly open. He watched her smile broaden with satisfaction...

And then she ate him.

Mr Ernest Quinn

Jacqueline Fletcher

Rosemary hurried through the lunchtime crowds. Such diversity in one high street: the window shoppers who aren't dictated to by bosses; the shopaholics whose masses of designer bags and carriers stab into your calves and bruise your shins; the one hour desperadoes trying to meet and eat; smart suited gentlemen who look as if they own the town and carry themselves with dignity, oozing charm, while the younger gents, although smart and handsome, seem too glib and arrogant, the young bucks.

She gave her heart to one of these, trusted her love and devotion to a handsome young buck. And whilst she was in a heavenly cloud, a heady vapour of perfume, soft words, tender lips, greedy hands and perspiration, he was bucking her best friend on Tuesday nights.

Her eyes stung as her tears threatened to turn her delicate, pretty features into a red-faced, champion gurner. No, no, no more crying. Be positive. Forget them. She had cried enough in the last six months.

Rosemary dashed into the shopping centre to her favourite café. It was a balcony café on the top floor and looked down on all the hundreds of shoppers, a theatre in the round.

She sat at her favourite table which was reserved for her between one and two o'clock.

Everything was ready: prawn salad sandwiches on brown with seafood sauce, a pot of tea for one and a small lemon tart. Oooh! Lovely. She eased off her shoes and settled back in the chair whilst pouring her tea. To her right was the rotunda, the stage of life. To her left was her favourite shop, *An Officer and A Gentleman*. The name gave her heart a warm feeling; she loved the film too. Very romantic.

She could see Ernest Quinn through the window. He was good looking and very smart. She had been in and bought a shirt last week and a lovely jumper the week before. They were still at home in the bags. She would have to stop making excuses and spending her money just to get closer to Ernest. 'You don't want your heart breaking again, Rosemary,' she would tell herself. Yet she knew you can't let a bad experience put you off. If at first you don't succeed...

Rosemary loved her job. It was full of drama, humour, romance and anything you wished. Being a librarian gave you a different life every day. You could be whatever you wanted.

Today she wanted to be decisive. She had a plan. At three o'clock she finished work and went straight to the shop. At four o'clock she reached her car, weighed down with carriers from *An Officer and a Gentleman*. It had been her turn to cripple shoppers. The handles were nearly slicing through her fingers, which had gone white and numb at the tips. Her arms and back ached, but she was so happy. Okay, it had cost her quite a bit, but it was worth every penny. Ernest Quinn had come to tea.

Rosemary wasn't a very tidy person, but tonight she had made an effort to quickly spruce up her apartment and place scented candles around the lounge. She hid all her parcels in the wardrobe. Her apartment was on the first floor and overlooked the local cricket club. She had often imagined them both sitting on her veranda sipping cocktails and watching the cricket – it was beautiful on summer evenings – and now here he was, doing just that!

Tonight was going to be a success. She didn't want to throw herself at him as she had with Max. She wanted to build up a relationship, enjoy getting to know each other. Take it slowly.

It was all going so well. *Too* well. Rosemary was just bringing in the cheese and biscuits when the door bell rang.

She looked through the tiny security glass and nearly screamed. There on the other side of the door stood Angela, the hussy, the ex-best friend, the boyfriend stealer, the Medusa on two legs. Rosemary felt her heart thumping in her chest, her throat tightened and she had difficulty breathing. What did that bitch want? She was going to ignore her when Angela banged on the door and shouted,

"I know you are in, Rosemary. Open the door."

Rosemary left the security chain on, opening the door just a fraction so she didn't need to face her enemy.

"Is that Max in there with you?" asked Angela.

"He most certainly isn't," said Rosemary. "There is no way he will ever see the inside of my apartment again."

"You've got company," said Angela waspishly. "How do I know it's not Max?"

"I am telling you it isn't. That's the truth and that's enough. Just leave now, thank you."

With that Rosemary shut the door, pleased that she hadn't demeaned herself by being rude but confused and bemused by the apparent ending of Max and Angela's romance.

She walked into the lounge and Ernest was still sitting on the veranda gazing over the cricket field with an enigmatic look on his face. She sat next to him and took hold of his hand for comfort. He never moved, but his hand did: it fell off. The movement made her jump as she was left with his cold, stiff fingers mingling with her own.

The tears that had gently sprung from her eyes were sliding slowly down her cheeks, and when she started to laugh, she couldn't stop. She felt hysterical. What a stupid, crazy mess. All she wanted was a bit of company without any complications. Ernest seemed ideal: handsome, well dressed and totally undemanding. He was her placebo.

Her stomach was aching with laughing so much. She couldn't get Ernest's hand back on properly, the sleeve of his shirt kept getting in the way.

"Right, Ernest, let's get you over to the settee and see what else drops off." She started to lift him off the chair and then slowly straightened him up. She didn't want him completely straight because he was going to sit down on the settee. She was hanging on to him like a novice on *Strictly Come Dancing*, slowly waltzing backwards, with her knees slightly bent. His feet must stay on the floor or a leg may drop off. She could feel the hysterical giggles bubbling in her stomach and chest again.

She wondered how Angela knew she had company. She hoped Angela couldn't see her with Ernest now; it wouldn't look normal to a voyeur. Or would it?

Ernest was, at last, sitting on the sofa. Rosemary was exhausted. Too much emotion for one day. "You can stay there for the night Ernest. I shall see you in the morning," she said.

She brought the table back into the lounge and closed the patio doors. Then just left everything as it was. That cheese would smell in the morning, but she couldn't care less. "Goodnight, Ernest," she smiled.

The alarm went off at seven-thirty A.M., but Rosemary hit the snooze button without even waking up. Fifteen minutes later the alarm went off again, which, thankfully, woke her this time, but what a rush she was in!

She kissed the top of Ernest's head, wishing she could look as smart and fresh in the mornings, and left the apartment in a tip.

The day passed fairly quickly. Lunch was strange today; no weaving romantic stories around Ernest. She had told the girls in the shop he was for a play she was producing. They didn't seem that interested in her, only the five hundred pounds it cost for him and some clothes.

She left work at four o'clock. An exhausted feeling invaded her body as she sat in the car.

Arriving home, she parked in her allotted space and skipped up the steps to her front door.

Feeling brighter, but realising she had a few jobs to do, she threw open the front door and stepped inside, shutting the door with her right foot in one practiced move, and prepared mentally for action.

There was something very different about her apartment. She could smell polish straight away. She walked slowly into the lounge. Ernest was still sat on the settee looking immaculate, all his limbs in place, but the room was spotless. All the washing up had been done, the pots put away, all surfaces tidied, wiped and polished. She went into the bedroom which looked like a showroom. She was sure the windows had been cleaned too. She kept looking at Ernest, trying to catch him moving. She checked everywhere and found the whole place had been transformed, as if Cinderella herself had been in for the day.

She stood in front of the settee staring at Ernest. Surely it couldn't have been him, her wonderful man, E. Quinn?

Everlasting Youth

Tamsyn Naylor

It was getting on towards night. The lengthening shadows crept into the valley from all sides and stole away the warmth of the sun's rays, leaving grey half-light to trick the eye and widen the senses. I needed to make a bed for the night, or at least some shelter to keep the damp off. Scratting around, I managed to find some sizable branches that could be propped up as a lean-to shelter; the warmth I created inside would be enough to keep us both comfortable. Although the car was not too far away, I had not had the foresight to put a blanket in the boot, or even a flask of coffee for all that. There were some crisps and nibbles and boiled sweets in the glove box, enough to tide us over until we found a shop in the morning, then I could be a bit more organised. A crude covering of bracken fronds stacked over the branches and an armful of mid-season leaf fall formed a dry, protective layer between us and the damp night.

Woken early by bird song, the valley before us slowly opened up to daylight, which entered over the rim and slowly slid down the hillside opposite until it reached the stream, before jumping over it and scampering about the rocks, looking for places to settle. It would be simple enough for me to put together a drink for breakfast from this water. If I stirred myself and made the effort to gather some dry sticks, we could even have it warmed. The dampness had seeped into my very being in this natural resting place.

Our day was spent around the watersides, reminiscing about childhood and mutual friends and the early times in our relationship. It was a simple time: no responsibilities and just each other to spend our waking hours and thoughts with. Every little thing was a big thing and, even though we had not known many earth-shattering experiences ourselves, all sorts of silly things that had happened to people we knew became part of the tapestry of our lives. We were well-known for slipping away spontaneously and losing ourselves somewhere for a few days, if the mood took us.

The valley was still and quiet, quite lazy. Sleep took over as we idled away the afternoon. The evening meal was welcome, its warm steam rising from above the pan and permeating our senses, a fine glass of wine complementing the simple stew and the flames from the fire dancing on our cheeks. I held her hand and kissed it, looking into her deep, soulful eyes and watching her wrinkles, from all the good times we'd had together, spider out from the corner of her lips.

The evening mist settled down with us, bending all the grass stems the way it wanted them and smoothing all the rocks to catch the shimmer of the half-moonlight above us. As the encroaching dew crept up from the river, it settled on spider webs, appearing like steam across a mirror, picking out words of a loved one. Clinging to the edges of the wood, the mist engulfed the carpet of stars, thinning out and eventually smothering the moon.

Breakfast the next morning quenched my appetite for the day ahead. Should it be a walk along the moor edge or just tinkering around at the riverside, watching for minnows or the dancing dragonfly? Just to be here with her was comfort itself, what else could we need in life?

Later, the afternoon sun lengthened, clouds gathered from the lip of the ravine, keeping pace with the trees before moving over to obscure the view and hemming us in to its whim. Why had no-one ever built a house here? I wondered. Maybe it's because it was difficult putting a track down there, or maybe it was just too far away from anywhere.

The breeze that sprang up was stiff and boisterous; I began to think it would be better to get back to the car, away from the austere feeling that had come about. A small amount of panic came over me but it was useless and uncalled for. Dusk was the time of day when time and place could be bent, irrational instincts were strong and all encompassing, the many thoughts played out throughout the day coming back to haunt the mind. Best just to sleep, even if only in short amounts; but tomorrow we really should move on.

The next day didn't really dawn, it just became light, a strange subdued light, not strong enough to seek out all the hidden spaces. Thoughts of food again took over; how about gathering a few berries to go with breakfast, or some mushrooms to cook over the fire? What had seemed to give me comfort previously now towered over me dauntingly, all warmth had gone. A cold shiver took hold. Reaching over to her, I stroked her pale, china-like face, smoothing hair caught in her mouth as she lay.

'We should get back to the car, love,' I said.

She did not respond. Our stay in this place was becoming stale; it was time to go home. I was exhausted; the damp had got into my bones to a point that I was helpless. Looking down at my legs, the twisted bone of my shin protruded, splintered and torn. The car was only metres away but it was smashed and upturned, beyond recognition; besides I had not the energy to reach it. I had no sensation of pain, just tingling from the top of my thigh. As light became night I sank between feelings of panic and calm, all the time a blackness coming over me.

Night came and my exhausted eyes closed to keep out the spectres. My hand held hers as we lay together beneath the all-seeing moon.

The Cottage

Paula Harrison

In my early days you were just the shell of a building with holes in the roof and no windows. Pigeons nested in the front room and soot covered the floor. Later, you were lit by candles and oil lamps and were kept warm by log fires. Water was brought in from the tap in the field, or from the river. The light from your windows pierced the black night on the moor as your smoke drifted upward into the frosty sky.

Even back then, you were from another era. Time had moved on but you hadn't, with your stone sink resting on bricks in a kitchen made from railway sleepers. You were isolated from the world and prying eyes.

The old washhouse stood proud in your grounds, smoke drifting from the chimney as first my Grandma and later my Mother toiled with the washing.

Time moved on but your protective stones shielded us from gales, blizzards and storms. When I was born, you were an old house. As I grew up I saw you change. Switches now turn lights on, and water comes through pipes. Gardens are now neatly lawned and cottage flowers grow in pretty beds. You were always productive as fruit and vegetables grew in your grounds.

All my life you have been my heaven, my haven of inner peace and a protective force. You have stood the test of time. Time that has moved on. You have sheltered us for four generations. Family members have become old, with impaired memory, but they still remember you. They smile when you are spoken about. The happy times you gave us bring comfort to confused minds; we have had the best of you. Soon you will be sold. Our ways will part and others will take on the role of being your guests, but I will never forget you. I will be the shadow on your wall, the moon shining on the river, the dew on the rose bush.

Riverside Cottage, thank you. In a few weeks I will kiss your stones goodbye. May history repeat itself, making you a sanctuary for another four generations. The Murk Esk will continue carving its course to be won by the sea; the trees will always stand proud on the river bank watching over you. The seasons will change. And you will always be indelibly printed in my mind.

The Last Supper

Delphine Gale

It's Friday morning, and the rain is battering the windows. The door slams as he leaves for work, the signal for my tears to start falling and I cannot control them. My coffee goes as cold as the rest of the house is now that the children have all left for bigger, brighter futures, but I take another sip anyway. I have to find a way to repair what is broken, so I dry my eyes with the back of my hand and resolve to salvage the day, which is in danger of being written off before it has even had a chance to start.

The weather girl on the radio (no longer a bleak white noise in the background) tells me that the rain will clear, leaving a warm, sunny afternoon and evening. Things will improve, she tells me. I believe her, and decide to help things along. I will try to get him back, this distant man of mine, from wherever he has been in his head these last few months. I will start by making his favourite dessert, an easy lemon concoction which almost defeats me even though I have made it a thousand times before. It doesn't though, and buoyed by my success I hoover and dust and prepare for when he comes home, when he will eat his favourite meal, have a glass of his favourite wine and come back to me once more, so we can be like we used to be when we were younger. I have to start somewhere. The memory of those distant days cheers me, the days when no-one in the world existed except the two of us, wrapped up in each other's arms, lives, very existence, when there was no room for anyone else and I worshipped him. I still do, my very own deity, strong, capable, handsome and clever. I am so lucky. Smiling now, I notice the first of the blue sky appearing, and the sunshine bit by bit chases away the sullen grey clouds until they sulk off over the horizon. The weather girl did not lie, and as I step outside, the promised warmth embraces me and I drink in the fresh, clean aroma left behind by the retreated rain.

We will have his favourite meal outside, I decide, bathed in the evening sun which cannot fail to be there because the weather girl said it would be. I notice our little stone patio covered in the debris of last week's gardening, and I hear his voice: "What the hell is all that mess?" so I resolve to clear it to the bonfire pile, once I have wiped over the table and chairs in readiness for our supper. Just us, like it always used to be, my god and I. I will try again to discover what is troubling him, and thus me. I haven't shared my concerns with the children; I am afraid, but I hope that he might – just might – say, "Oh you silly thing, have I really been so distant? Well I'm sorry to have worried you. I am fine," and he will take me in his big strong arms and kiss me tenderly and the world will be right again. He won't be ill, as I imagine him to be, and the business will not be failing terribly as I imagine it is. These are the only things that would affect him so badly that his eyes are empty and his face cold, closed and distant, his frozen back turned to me every night when I climb into bed beside him, resisting my every attempt to thaw him back into my arms and into his heart. I will do this; I will mend whatever is broken with the sheer weight of the love I have for him.

I pick up the pile of garden detritus in my arms, and take it down the little stones steps, to the bonfire pile, out of sight. Nothing will spoil this evening, not even the rubbish. As I carefully negotiate the mossy steps I slip, and, unable to stay upright, fall heavily against the low stone wall. My legs crumple beneath me and my arms are unable to save me. I feel a blinding pain in my head and bright light sears my brain. I can feel something warm and sticky against my face before everything goes black and still. I have no idea how long I am lying here. In the distance I see a small bright light, very small, a pin prick really, but I have an overwhelming urge to fight against its approach, to be with him. I feel cold now, in spite of the afternoon sun, and have a desperate need for help. As the blackness slowly recedes, save for the pin prick of light, I can see that storm clouds seem to be gathering, and I realise the weather girl lied after all. All my senses are dim and it feels as though I am floating a little. In the distance, I think I can hear a car and my heart gives a little beat. Is it him? The car comes closer and I hear the tyres on the gravel. It is him! It must be! I hear what I think must be footsteps, but everything is so muffled, so distant. My heart soars as I realise it is him. I am lifted. Literally lifted, as, looking down, I now see my injured self on the little steps, bloodied face and head smashed against the wall where I fell. No matter, he is here now and I am saved. He gets out of the car and goes into the house, through the front door I have left open. He shouts, increasingly annoyed at my silence. I shout back, "I am here, my love!" but he does not hear. He comes back to the door, hand sliding through dishevelled hair, frustration at my absence. "Where the hell have you got to?" he shouts angrily, but I know the anger will go when he finds me. He comes across the patio, past the clean table and chairs with the waiting tablecloth fluttering idly in the breeze.

He crosses the grass and finds me. "What are you doing?" he says impatiently, then realises what has happened. I watch him bend over me and I long for his touch which would heal my injuries, but he does not touch me, or reach out to me. I am drawn to the heat emanating from him, and notice the small distant light is getting brighter and bringing with it its own heat. I need heat, I am desperate to rid myself of the cold but I fight against the light. He stands now, and looking over me gets out his phone. He is going to call an ambulance. He looks at his phone but does not unlock it or dial. He merely checks the time and I follow him back to the house. Inside, he scans the meal I have prepared in the kitchen but his face does not soften or betray anything. He pauses, and I throw my arms around him: "It's ok, I am here, I am better! Sorry for my accident. I didn't want to put you to any trouble," but he does not hear my words or feel my embrace; he just shivers violently. I gently stroke his face with my fingers, searching for the love that was once there but he brushes his cheek with irritation.

I am crying now, the heat from him is weaker and although I am desperate to reach it I cannot. I follow him upstairs, my last chance, and he goes into our bedroom. Our sanctuary. I will reach him here, I can feel the undiluted love of our marriage in this room. He goes to his drawer, rummages, and from a redundant shaver case takes out a phone. He has another phone! The first one must not be working and he will ring for the ambulance. He dials. I am saved. Someone picks up at the other end and as he turns and looks me straight in the eyes I see that the softness is back and the cold distance banished, his face and his dark brown beautiful eyes are again filled with love.

"Hi," I hear him say, with that gentle voice returned and overflowing with affection. "You won't believe what happened. We're going to be alright. I love you!" The heat returns all around him, but it is not for me.

The distant light is upon me now, I am unable to resist its allure any longer. Its gentle warmth wraps itself around me and I am comforted like never before. Slowly the light is replaced by a soothing velvet darkness which consumes me, but I am not afraid. I understand.

Spots of rain begin to fall from the now dark clouds. He redials a number and as I hear him say "Ambulance please, my wife has had an accident and I think she may be dead," I cannot maintain the struggle to be with him any longer and I slip from his life forever. My Apollo.

Half a Hero

Antony Wootten

When he heard the key in the lock, John took a deep breath, forced a smile, straightened his jumper – swearing silently as he noticed a ketchup stain on it – and turned to face the door.

"Yes, Mum," Gloria was saying into her phone, crossly, as she entered the flat. "Yes, I know. No, I won't. Mum, I'm here now. I've got to go. Bye." She put the phone away in her pocket and shut the door behind her with her foot. Her overnight rucksack on her back, she said, "Hi Dad," and dropped her schoolbag on the floor.

"Hello, love," John said, stepping towards her a little uncertainly. He began to open his arms to embrace her, but he could see her smile was a forced, polite one. She didn't really want to be here. She wanted to be at home with her mum and her superhero stepdad. Or out shopping with her mates, or something. So John aborted the hug before it had even begun and diverted his trajectory towards the schoolbag, which he scooped up and hugged instead. "Gonna be great to have my little girl here for the weekend," he said, his voice slightly higher than he'd intended. Why was he so nervous of Gloria these days?

"I'm not a little girl," Gloria managed.

"No, I know, I..." he said, and tailed off.

"Sorry," she said, quickly.

"It's alright, love. I was thirteen once too you know."

"I'm fourteen," she corrected him.

"Yes, sorry, yes, fourteen," he said hurriedly. "That's what I meant. I..."

"I'm going to get changed," she said, and walked past him to her bedroom.

"Okay, love. Want a cuppa?" John said, but the door was shut before he'd even finished the question. He stood looking at the blank white surface of the door which was punctuated by long, shiny bumps where the paint had run, like teardrops. His arms tightly round the bag, he rocked very slightly from side to side, like a little boy hugging a teddy bear.

His flat was a small council flat on the thirtieth floor of an old tenement. It consisted of two bedrooms, a bathroom, and a lounge-diner with the kitchen at one end. He wished he could offer Gloria more than this. He wished he could afford something big and ostentatious, like the palatial mansion where Gloria lived with her mum and Captain Stratosphere. But here, the mildewed wallpaper was peeling, the front room carpet was threadbare, and, although the flat was small and Gloria could never be more than a few feet away, she was already beyond a closed door, and might as well be in a different country. However, just as he was about to turn away, the door opened and Gloria peered out. "Yes please," she said quietly, before closing it again.

Once the kettle was boiling, he emptied Gloria's bag, pulled on his rubber gloves and started washing her lunchbox. As he did so he gazed out of the window across the misty city. The sun was low, and the haze was bronze in the west, fading to grey blue twilight in the east. Birds wheeled, and in the distance a couple of superheroes sped to where they were needed: a crime scene, or an accident perhaps. John envied them. How wonderful it must be to leap into the air and zoom upwards, with no need of a plane or a helicopter or special flying suit, to swoop down into the city, rescuing people and apprehending criminals. Perhaps that would give Gloria a reason to be proud of him.

He heard Gloria emerging from her room. He turned, and she seemed to hesitate in the doorway. There was something in her hand; a mug, John realised. She came towards him, head down, as if she had a guilty secret. "What's wrong, love?" John asked.

"Nothing," she said, coming closer. "Nothing. It's... nothing." But John could tell what it was. She was worried he was going to hug her. It tortured him that she had become so withdrawn, so afraid of physical contact with her own father. Still, who could blame her? He was such a disappointing father.

She gave him an awkward smile, and took over

making the tea. That was when he saw that the mug had a picture of Captain Stratosphere – her stepfather – on it. "Oh, that's nice," John said trying to sound sincere and un-offended.

"Sorry," she said.

"No, love. It's fine. You use it. He's a good man."

"He gave it to me."

"Well, that's kind of him," John said. Gloria nodded. John pulled his washing-up gloves off and batted away the soap suds that fluttered into his face as the rubber twanged. He dropped them into the sink.

"Do you still take five sugars, Dad?" Gloria asked, taking the lid off the sugar jar.

"Yeah," he said. "Just the five. I'm on a health kick."

"Very funny," she said.

They took their mugs of tea and went to sit down.

"So, um, love..." John said. Gloria looked at him. "Um... What do you want to do this weekend, eh? I thought maybe we could go ice skating. You love ice skating."

"I'm going to meet up with my friends tomorrow," she said.

"Oh." He took another slurp of tea. "Doing anything nice?"

"Well, Lisa's just found out her dad's got a superpower, so—"

"Has he?" John said. "What, Colin Smith? *That* Lisa?"

"Yep."

"God, he was such a squirt at school. What's his superpower then? Who is he? Have I heard of him?"

"He can go invisible," Gloria explained. "He hasn't ever bothered with a superhero name and costume and all that stuff because no-one can see him anyway, and he wanted to keep out of the public eye. He foiled a bank robbery last week, but he got shot in the process."

"Shot?" John gasped. "Is he alright?"

"Yes. He's alright, but some annoying paparazzi bloke followed the trail of blood and found out about him. Didn't you see it in the paper?"

"I don't look at the paper much."

"Anyway," Gloria said, "he's been outed. Everyone knows who he is now. So I'm going to meet him and see him go invisible."

"Invisible," John breathed, and took a sip of tea."Hey," he said as something occurred to him. "His invisibility... Does it... Does it make his clothes go invisible too, or does he have to..."

"Does he have to take his clothes off?" Gloria finished for him. "Not sure. Never asked. I'll find out tomorrow."

"Not sure I'm happy about that," John said.

"I'm only joking, Dad. Don't worry. His clothes go invisible too. He doesn't need to get naked. Wouldn't matter if he did though; he'd be invisible."

"Yes, invisible and naked," John nodded

portentously. He shuddered, and changed the subject. "Now that he's been outed, is he going to have a persona? What's he going to call himself?"

Gloria sipped her tea. "What's on telly?" she asked, reaching for the control.

"Gloria?" John said, sensing her reluctance to answer his question. He put his mug down and leaned forwards. "What's he called?"

"It doesn't matter what he's called."

"Well, clearly it does, otherwise you'd tell me."

Gloria just tutted, and turned the TV on.

"Come on, love. It's only a name. Why on earth wouldn't you want me to know it? I'll find out sooner or later on the news anyway."

Gloria sighed. "Ghost Man," she said. "Sorry, Dad."

"Ghost Man?" John cried in dismay, throwing his arms up and falling backwards into his chair. "That was going to be my name!"

"I know. But you don't have a super power, Dad," Gloria said, thumbing through the channels.

"I nearly do, love. You know that."

"Yes, but..."

John nodded. "But it's a rubbish one. That's what you were going to say."

"Well, no," Gloria said. "It's not a rubbish superpower. It's not a superpower at all. It's a disability."

John looked at her.

"Isn't it?" she stated, hammering home the point. "It's why you can't hold down a job. It's why you live here." She could be so cruel sometimes. But she was right.

"I know, love," he said. "I know." He took an extra long gulp of tea, and let the mug engulf his face, hiding his embarrassment for a few moments. At last, he had to put it down though. "The ability to walk through walls would be a truly great superpower," he said with an awkward smile. "If I could walk through walls I could sneak into and out of anywhere. I could spy on criminals in their lairs and catch them red handed, carrying out their evil plans."

"Yep," Gloria said.

But John couldn't walk through walls though. Not properly, anyway. Not easily enough for it to be a useful superpower. He could, when no-one was looking, push himself slowly through thin walls and doors, but it was an enormous effort and took him hours of straining and concentrating to do it. It felt like pushing himself through a giant wine gum. And it was humiliating to be found stuck there, floundering, his back in one room and his front in another.

He'd been caught like that before, when he was a teenager. A sixteen year old would-be-chocolate-thief stuck in the wall of the sixth form tuck shop was, for the three lads who found him, an irresistible opportunity for mischief. He'd been going through the wall backwards so he could see anyone coming, even though a quick getaway would have been out of the question. Inevitably, the lads who found him there, lodged half way through the wall and unable to extricate himself without a huge amount of effort, drew penises on his face and cut his hair. Then, they found the prefect who ran the tuck shop, got the key from her and let themselves in. John's back end was already inside, and they filled his trousers with so much chocolate it looked as if he'd messed himself. They then went round the school inviting anyone and everyone to come and marvel at their creativity.

That was twenty or so years ago, but, not surprisingly, he was still scarred by the experience. Worse still, the ability to pass through solid objects would sometimes manifest itself by making him sink, involuntarily, a little way into a surface he was in contact with. He would then be stuck there until he managed to slowly pull himself free. That could be a real problem. A danger even. Once, his hand sank into the steering wheel of the car, and his elbow into the arm rest on the door. Suddenly, he'd been unable to steer. The result was a spectacular crash. The car had rolled into a lake. Gloria, eleven at the time, was in the back, and her mother – John's then wife – was in the passenger seat. The memory filled John with a sickening guilt. He had almost killed his family. But Stratosphere Man, who was blessed with many fully-functioning superpowers, had appeared from nowhere and rescued them all, pulling the car to bits with his bare hands. Who could blame Gloria's mother for falling madly in love with such a gallant and handsome hero?

"You're hanging onto that mug as if your life depends on it," John observed. The picture of Captain Stratosphere seemed to be grinning at him. "Mine's gone cold. Want another?"

Gloria shook her head. Then she changed her mind. "Yeah, I'll do it though," she said.

"It's alright, love," John assured her, standing. "I'm not an invalid. Give it here, I'll do it."

"No," she said sharply. She stood and took his mug from the coffee table. "I'll do it. You order the pizza."

"If you're sure," he said, watching her all the way to the kettle, as if he was worried she'd not find the way. She didn't reply as she started making the drinks. "Can't believe he's called himself Ghost Man," John said, half to himself as he reached for the phone and sat back down. "That was always going to be my name, the bloody sod."

*

A short while later, a shadow spread across the room as the evening sunlight was obscured by the fluttering arrival of a presence on the balcony.

"Ah, pizzas," John said cheerfully, and he heaved himself out of his chair. He opened the balcony door, and there stood the imaginatively named Pizza Delivery Man. "Hello, mate," John said, relieving the red-faced youngster of the two flat boxes.

Pizza Delivery Man stood there with his hands

on his hips, trying to create the archetypal superhero silhouette, but it was clear that his muscles were just foam padding. A couple of them had slipped slightly out of place, and the wiriness of his limbs was obvious.

"That'll be fourteen pounds please," Pizza Delivery Man said in a voice with hero-style depth and volume. But it was unnatural for him and he had to clear his throat afterwards.

As John emptied a jar of notes and coins onto the kitchen worktop, Gloria, from the sofa, looked at Pizza Delivery Man and said, "That's the best use of your power, do you think?"

"What's it got to do with you?" he objected, not bothering trying to make his voice sound booming anymore. He adjusted his mask, which had slipped a little. It was designed to look like two slices of pepperoni, one over each eye. "Don't give me that *with great power comes great responsibility* nonsense," he said. "I don't want the responsibility. There are enough superheroes in this city, don't you think? I'm only seventeen. I haven't decided what I want to do. Right now, I just want to party. I'm doing this to save up some money so I can go to uni."

"Oh yes?" John said, returning with a fistful of money. "What're you going to study?"

"Dunno," the lad replied. "Accountancy, probably."

"Accountancy?" John said as he handed over the cash. "Don't you want to make use of your power? You're incredibly lucky. You can fly!" he said dreamily. "Just think of the things you could do with that power."

"Yes, but I've still got to earn a living, mate, just like everyone else. It's only the really successful superheroes who make a living at it, your Jet Mans and your Mighty Womans. Maybe I don't want to catch criminals. Maybe I'd be no good at it. Oh," he said, his attention caught by something. "That's Captain Stratosphere, isn't it?" He was looking at the mug Gloria was still holding.

Gloria nodded. "He's my stepdad," she explained, sheepishly.

"He's your... No way!"

Suddenly, in the distance beyond the jagged skyline of spires and towers, there was a flash of orange light, and a mushroom of fire billowed into the sky. Pizza Delivery Man ducked and emitted a high-pitched squeal. "What the hell...?" John said craning to see past him. A moment later came the noise, a low, moaning burble: the sound of an explosion muffled by distance.

"What was that?" Gloria said, jumping to her feet and joining John at the balcony door.

Pizza Delivery Man straightened. He looked flustered and pale. "Whatever it was," he said, "I'm sure the heroes can handle it." John nodded in agreement. The fireball had dissipated, and a thick, dark smudge of smoke climbed slowly above where it had been. The moon was almost full, and was beginning to glow brightly over the city. The first few stars were twinkling as daylight receded.

"Anyway," John said, "keep the change." That seemed to cheer the lad up.

"Thanks mate," he said. "Have a great evening." With that, he leapt off the balcony, and John and Gloria watched him soar into the darkening sky.

"What made that noise, Dad?" Gloria asked. "Did you see anything? Was it an explosion?" It wouldn't have been the first time Gloria had heard an explosion. In her short life, the city had come under attack from evil forces several times. The superheroes had seen off the attackers on every occasion, but Gloria had seen her fair share of violence and destruction. John hoped this was not the beginning of another attack. He was about to reassure her, telling her it was nothing, when three huge helicopters thundered right past the block some distance below their balcony. "Woah!" Gloria gasped as they watched the machines weave between buildings until they were out of sight. John had to admit, this was not looking good. "Dad," Gloria breathed, and she looked up at him with wide, frightened eyes. "I think it's happening again!"

Just then, two more fireballs rose above the horizon almost simultaneously. Three more followed, and several more after that. When the noise reached them, it was like rocks rolling down a mountain. Beyond nearby buildings, low and stealthy, more helicopters could be heard but not seen. A great flock of flying superheroes suddenly soared overhead, and several others swung from building to building beneath them, hurrying towards the action.

"Quick, pop the telly on, love," John said as they blundered their way back inside the flat. Her hands shaking, Gloria fumbled for the control, dropped it, scooped it up and tried again. The TV flashed into life. The words 'Emergency Broadcast' filled a strip at the bottom of the screen, and the camera was shakily trying to focus on a female reporter who, whilst forcing her way against the flow of fleeing crowds along a wide street in the financial district, was giving a running commentary: "It started just a few minutes ago, with no warning. There have been several explosions – more than I could count – oh! Another one!" The reporter ducked behind a car, the camera juddering as its operator dropped down behind her. Around them, people were screaming and diving into doorways as smoke and debris billowed down the street. The microphone picked up the sound of stones and shrapnel pinging against the car. The reporter, turning to the camera conspiratorially, said, "We must be getting close. Stay tuned. I guarantee we will be the first to bring you footage of..." As she spoke, the shaking camera panned past her, street lamps flaring in its lens as it zoomed in on a huge, dark shape as tall as towerblock, looming through the dispersing smoke. As it came into focus, the reporter gasped. The towering silhouette, vaguely humanoid and with red, glowing eyes, now filled the shot. Suddenly, the people who had been sheltering from the previous explosion broke their cover, and the street was filled with a cacophony of screaming and shouting which came through the TV's speaker in distorted crackles. The camera moved in a way which suggested that the videographer who was holding it was about to join them, but the reporter hissed, "Stay down, you idiot." Above them, the red eyes glowed brighter and from them there suddenly came two beams of light which, for an instant, made the screen white-out. The camera adjusted itself to the brightness just in time to capture several people exploding into tiny, smoking fragments of flesh and bone, raincoat and brogue. A pair of glasses skittered to the pavement right in front of the camera, and the videographer couldn't resist zooming in on them in artistic poignancy.

Then, the camera panned upwards again, and, over the reporter's shoulder, showed the titanic, red-eyed beast, much closer now, standing there scanning the streets and buildings. Wisps of smoke and wind-born fragments fluttered before it. The camera's microphone picked up the sound of the reporter's breathing. The crowds had fallen silent, or disappeared completely. The reporter turned to the camera, whispering determinedly: "What it is, who can tell? It seems to be a metallic structure, a robot of some kind. Just when we thought this city had seen it all, this incredible monster, and many others like it, have emerged from the oceans and..." Behind her, a huge, mechanical foot rose as the beast took a giant step. Sensing this, the reporter froze, still facing the camera, her eyes wide, and sweat beading on her forehead. She was holding her breath now. She gestured to the videographer to be silent, but the mic picked up the sound of wheezing hyperventilation from behind the camera. The ground shook as the foot, which was as big as a house, thumped down onto the street. The other foot rose and swung towards them, filling the frame. The reporter turned to look, just in time to see the foot's underside blotting out the sky. "Run!" she shrieked, and the camera swung wildly as they scrambled belatedly to their feet. There was a cry, darkness, and a storm of static snow filled the screen. The news desk appeared and a white and wide-eyed anchorman said, "Um... We seem to have lost the link..."

John and Gloria looked at each other. "Are they dead?" Gloria asked quietly. John could not refute the suggestion, yet he didn't want to admit it either, so he just stared back at her and was grateful for the sound of her mobile ringing. One hand still gripping her mug, Gloria pulled the phone from her pocket with the other. "Hello? Mum! Are you alright? Yes, yes, I'm fine. I'm here with Dad. What? No, I'm not... no. Mum. No. Mum. Mum, listen. I'm not leaving Dad. Mum!"

From outside, an almost ambient roar had been

building, practically un-noticed by John and Gloria, a growing cacophony of explosions which merged into a single wall of sound, getting closer and louder all the time.

Out of the dark sky, a figure sped towards them, its cape flapping wildly as it approached at great speed. Involuntarily, John emitted an audible tut as he realised who this was. A moment later, standing there on the balcony, looking amazing in his green lycra suit and orange cape which flapped in the wind like a flag, was Gloria's stepfather, Captain Stratosphere.

"Derek!" Gloria said, surprised but not altogether delighted. Into her phone, she told her mum, "I'm not going with him, Mum. No. I'm staying here with Dad."

"No, love," John said. "Go with him. Go on. He'll get you to safety."

John and Captain Stratosphere looked at each other and nodded.

"Alright, John?" said Captain Stratosphere.

"Alright, Derek?" said John.

"Hey, glad you like the mug!" Captain Stratosphere commented, pointing proudly at the novelty Gloria was still holding. "You seen that, John?" he enquired, grinning. John nodded, and wished his daughter would get rid of the sodding thing.

"It's nice," John managed.

"Mum, I've got to go," Gloria said. "Yes, Derek's here. Yes. Yes. I love you too. Bye." She slid the phone into her pocket.

"I can take Gloria," Captain Stratosphere explained, "but I'll have to come back for you, John. You're a bit too... you know... *weighty*, even for me."

"I'm not coming, Derek," Gloria said.

Taken aback, Captain Stratosphere said, "You'll have to. Your mother insisted. I can't go back without you. She'll kill me." Behind him, explosions flashed and boomed. Captain Stratosphere seemed suddenly distracted by the television, and John noticed him roll his eyes in annoyance. Following his gaze, John saw the live footage of superheroes engaged in deadly combat with giant red-eyed robots. Strange, flying creatures had also joined the fray, but on which side, John couldn't tell. One of the superheroes had come out of the battle for a brief interview with a reporter.

"It's Colin," said John.

"Ghost Man," said Captain Stratosphere with a bit of a disgruntled sneer. "He gets everywhere at the moment. The media love him, just because he got himself shot."

"Are you going to rescue my daughter or not, Derek?" John said a little tetchily.

"I'm staying with you, Dad," Gloria objected. "I don't need rescuing."

John looked at her. He'd not expected her to react like that. But Captain Stratosphere sniggered and said, "Really?"

"Have you got something to say, Derek?" John snapped at the green-clad superhero. "Do you think I can't look after my own daughter?"

But Captain Stratosphere shushed him and pointed at the TV. Across the bottom of the screen, the words 'Important Information for Superheroes' were flashing. Ghost Man was recounting turning himself invisible and climbing up the outside of one of the colossal robots. Apparently, he'd already discovered there was some sort of power unit inside their abdomens. He was now imploring all superheroes to "target the upper abdomen. I couldn't get inside, but I could see through holes in the armour, and I saw a power cell the likes of which I've never seen before. Some of you might be powerful enough to break through the armour cladding. The military must target it with their missiles. If you can get inside, disconnect the power cell and you'll disable the machine." Ghost Man didn't have a special suit, he was just dressed in a shirt and jeans. His shirt was torn and his face was blackened by smoke. "It's gonna be tough," he added, "because of those mechanical bats that are protecting them. They are really nasty. Got to go," he said, and the camera tracked him as he ran towards the noise and chaos and became invisible, reporters bombarding him with questions as he went.

"Mechanical bats?" John gasped.

Suddenly, a huge mechanical bat with a wing-span the size of a Cessna swooped into view behind Captain Stratosphere, wrapped its mighty claws round his arms, and pulled him from the balcony.

"Derek!" John shouted, but he was unable to move. Both his feet had sunk into the living room floor and were stuck there. He and Gloria watched, helpless, as the bat carried the struggling Captain Stratosphere off into the night where explosions tore at the sky and fire illuminated the bellies of the clouds.

At last, Gloria said shakily, "Dad, we have to go. It's not safe here."

"Why didn't you go with Derek?" John asked.

"Did you not see the mechanical bat?" Gloria exclaimed, waving her hand towards where her step father had been standing.

"I know, but, that was after you'd said..."

"I dunno, Dad, but come on. We've got to..." Her voice tailed off as she realised her dad's predicament. She had seen this sort of thing happen to him many times before, particularly when he was stressed. Every time he and her mum had had a row, he'd ended up stuck to the floor, or the chair he was sitting in, or with his fist lodged in the kitchen worktop he had punched. And she knew that's what had caused the car crash. "You're stuck, aren't you," she stated, disdainfully.

John nodded. Memories of the crash flooded his mind; shame surged through his belly. "You go, love," he said. "I'll sort myself out." The battle raged outside like violent waves around a lighthouse, and the flat shuddered.

"I'm not going," Gloria said, shaking her head morosely. She stood there looking forlorn and helpless.

"Okay," John said, realising he couldn't force her to go. She was probably safer in here than anywhere else now anyway. And besides, he desperately wanted her near him. "Well, at least put that ruddy mug down please. I'm sick of the sight of Captain Stratosphere."

"Bit insensitive, Dad," Gloria said, "after what's just happened to him." But she smiled. She was joking. They both knew Captain Stratosphere would probably be alright, with his super-strength and his indestructability. Gloria moved towards him, the cup still in her hand. "Trouble is," she said, "I can't put it down. Look." She opened her fingers and turned her hand palm-down, but the cup didn't fall.

"What...?" John began, but he knew what this meant. He could see her hand wasn't just stuck to the mug; it had partially sunk into the pottery, fusing with it, just like the way his feet had fused with the floor, and his hand had once fused with the steering wheel. "Oh, love," he said with warm sorrow in his voice.

"I don't want to be like you," Gloria said. John blinked. There were tears in his eyes. "I don't want a disability like yours. I want a job, and a normal life."

"I'm really sorry," John breathed, his throat

tightening. He didn't want his daughter to be like him either.

"I hate this fucking mug," Gloria said suddenly. It was the first time John had ever heard her swear. "I was trying to put it in the bin this morning but it was stuck to my hand. I've been carrying it round all day. All my friends think I love it. I didn't want you to see it. But I didn't want you to know what was happening to me either, so I just, sort of... Sorry."

"Oh, love. You don't need to apologise to me. Is this the first time something like that has happened?"

Gloria shook her head. "It's been happening a lot."

"Well, don't worry. Maybe it'll become a fully-developed superpower. Give it time."

"Yeah," Gloria said, her voice swamped by a roar as a flash of fire lit up the sky. A hot wind whipped around the room from the open balcony door, ruffling Gloria's hair, but neither of them reacted to it. "It won't though. That's not how it works." That was true. Superpowers arrived fully-developed from the outset, usually in teenagers. If your superpower was weak when it arrived, that was how it would stay. And if it caused you problems, it always would. You could become skilled at deploying your superpower, but you couldn't make it stronger or stop it from behaving erratically, if that's what it did.

Then, Gloria did something she'd not done for a

very long time. She put her arms around her dad and pressed her face into his chest. "I'm sorry I'm horrible sometimes," she said.

John wrapped her in his arms and kissed the top of her head.

At that moment, there was a clatter. Gloria straightened and looked at her hand. She had dropped the mug. "Why couldn't that have happened this morning?" she said with a smile.

John was aware that something inside him had suddenly changed. He felt different. Physically. Instinctively, he knew his feet were no longer stuck in the floor. His mind was racing. He had heard about this sort of thing. "Love," he said, give me your hands." He held out his own. "Go on," he urged, as a lump of shrapnel smashed through the kitchen window and embedded itself in the opposite wall. Slowly, Gloria raised her hands above his, and tiny green sparks began to dance between them. Her eyes wide, she gazed up at her father. John, realising what was happening, felt a hot tear break and roll down his cheek. Gloria lowered her hands into his. Bright sparks swirled around them like emerald dust, and a pale green light emanated from all over their bodies.

"No way," Gloria said, amazed. "What's happening, Dad? Who's causing it? You or me?"

"I don't know," John said. All he knew was that his whole body seemed to tingle with power, a power he felt he understood fully and could control perfectly. This must be what those lucky few feel like on the morning they wake up to discover they have a superpower and are no longer ordinary. "It's amazing. Look." They both looked at his feet. He bent one knee and lowered his other leg down through the carpet as if dipping it in water. He withdrew it easily. Gloria copied his action, and laughed.

"Maybe you've got two superpowers," John hypothesised. That would not be wholly unusual. Captain Stratosphere had several. "Maybe one of your superpowers is to enhance other people's superpowers."

"Maybe yours is," she suggested.

"Maybe it's both of us," John said, barely able to get the words out. "Must be."

The sounds of battle seemed distant now, even though the fighting was closer than ever. The building shook as something exploded nearby. Bits of hot debris zipped through the air, breaking windows, smashing plaster from the walls, and passing right through John and Gloria without touching them.

"Are you thinking what I'm thinking?" Gloria asked.

"Yes," grinned John, "if you're thinking, 'Holy *fucking* Jesus Christ!'"

"Well, yes, Dad, but I'm also thinking—"

"The city's under attack, and we've got a superpower. We should go and help."

"Exactly."

"I can't fucking wait!"

"Stop swearing, Dad."

"Sorry, love."

Gripping Gloria's hand, he led the way to the door. Automatically, he went to open it, but then realised that, for the first time in his life, he would not need to. Hand in hand, they walked right through it. The stairwell was rammed with fleeing residents, but John and Gloria moved through them like ghosts, and as they went, they left a wake of cheers and whoops, applause and shouts of encouragement.

The ground floor was strewn with broken glass the burning wreckage of furniture and fittings. Smoke and darkness filled the normally well-lit lobby, but John and Gloria walked out into the street unhindered. Looking up, they saw a sky filled with superheroes, mechanical bats, military helicopters and planes. Lumps of rubble and girders fell from buildings. Ash and dust swirled in thick blizzards. And along the street came a robot like the one they'd seen on the television.

"Are you sure about this?" John said, knowing that they shared an understanding of what they had to do. Gloria nodded, grinning in fear and delight. The robot, distracted by its attackers, stomped erratically along the road, flipping and crushing cars with its gigantic feet. Red beams of fiery menace shot from its eyes, but they were directed skyward, not groundward. Helicopters fell, sky-scrapers crumbled, and John and Gloria stood unnoticed in the robot's path. They watched as one great metal foot rose, swayed above them filling the sky, and descended right on top of them. The flat underside of the appendage arrived on the tarmac of the street with an almighty crunch, but John and Gloria passed through its thickness into the dark cavern inside the foot. The space was lit only by the green light they emitted. Mechanical joints and cable-like tendons creaked as the beast's weight was transferred to the newly-planted foot. Above them, they could see up the inside of the leg towards the knee, like looking up a vast chimney. They climbed.

The beast's weight shifted as a giant step was taken, and soon the foot rose again. Inertia pulled at John and Gloria, but they clung tight to the leg's internal structure. Some gaps were too narrow for normal humans to pass through, but the pair were true superheroes now; as long as they were touching, solid matter was no hindrance to them. They found they could control their powers in subtle ways, parts of their bodies passing through solid obstacles even as their hands gripped others and their feet pushed. In places, it became impossible to climb whilst holding the other's hand. Their power stopped working when they let go of each other, but the glow remained, fading as the gap between them grew, so they stayed closed, joining hands when they could, and helping each other clamber through the knee joint, up the thigh to the hip joint, and on into the abdomen.

Here, they found themselves in a cavernous

space, and in its centre was an orb the size of a small car. It glowed red, sending a column of brilliant fire directly upwards, through the thorax and, presumably, into the head to power the robot's brain and the weapons in its eyes. This must be the source of the power that Ghost Man had mentioned. They had to disable it. Many cables and tubes snaked across the floor and up into the orb, the whole arrangement looking like a small tree. John and Gloria found the cables came away fairly easily, and they disconnected as many as they could. From the tubes came hissing jets of gas, and the ends of the cables sparked and leapt like spitting snakes.

Above them, the red column of fire – far from dying – glowed brighter and hotter. It became pink, then blue, then an intense stream of white energy.

"What have we done?" Gloria cried over the roar of the robot's internal workings and the raging battle beyond its armoured skin.

Something glowing dropped from above and hissed onto the floor. Realising what it was, John grabbed Gloria. More glowing blobs of molten metal were falling now like lava thrown from a volcano. Without a word passing between them, John and Gloria gripped each other's hands and ran at the outer wall. They leapt through it and were suddenly out in the cold night air, many stories high above street level. They fell past the robot's waist, past its knee, and down to the broken tarmac of the road. But they didn't stop there. They passed through the road, through the cold earth beneath and emerged a moment later in the dark, stuffy cavity of an underground station. They dropped to the cold concrete of the platform, and sank into it as if it were a cushioned bed. Just their faces and toes protruding above the platform's surface, they lay there, blinking up at the red emergency-lighting above them. The place was deserted. They both pulled themselves up out of the platform and stood there, looking at each other.

After several long, deep breaths, Gloria said, "O-M-G. Did it work?"

"I don't know. Let's go and see," John replied.

The station was closed and the gates were across, but they held hands and passed through them, emerging cautiously at street level a few moments later. The battle still raged, but the robot, which towered above them, was motionless. A lava flow of molten metal had tumbled from its side, run down its leg, and was now puddling around its feet, black scabs forming on the glowing liquid as it cooled.

"We did it," John said.

"We did it," Gloria echoed, and they hugged in celebration. As he held his daughter, John worried about what all this would mean for Gloria. Together, their superpower was complete, and wonderful, and useful, but he couldn't explain why. And he would not be there for her forever.

What would she do when he was gone, or even when he was not there with her on a daily basis?

But none of that mattered right now. The ground shook with the approaching footsteps of another giant robot. The air rippled with the shockwaves of countless explosions. Superheroes and mechanical bats soared overhead in intense dogfights, and John and Gloria had a part to play.

Ladykiller

Delphine Gale

"Thank you *so* much." His silky voice gently washed the words over the committee. "Now, moving on if you *don't* mind." Jane recognised the chairman's signal that the item in question was now at an end. She shifted in her seat, and cast another glance at the agenda. Not that it mattered. The agenda was just a list of numbered items, allegedly for discussion. She wasn't even sure their esteemed chairman knew what 'discussion' meant anymore. Still, it didn't matter, this was her last meeting. She was jumping ship.

Jane had been on the parish council for many years, starting when her eldest had started school. Robin James had been chairman even then, had charmed her into applying when a place became available, easing her into the work involved, and, she had to admit, making her feel special at a time when she had needed it most. She had suggested her husband take on the role, but he was too busy at work. Jane gazed distractedly around the old village hall, then idly turned the page of the agenda, doodling in the corner of page two. Gone were the days when she assiduously noted every comment, every nuance of every argument. She had been marking time for a while now. Jane looked round at the rest of the committee. Like her, most of them had been there for years, and they all had the same look of defeat.

"But I've said this before, it's impossible to do." His words slipped around the table, soporific monotone dragging at her eyelids as Robin James continued, "We just can't manage to accommodate a request such as this. Now, moving on, if you *don't* mind." Even the secretary had an air of battered resignation about him. Jane crossed her legs, uncrossed them, and admired her new shoes, then shifted her attention to the chairman. Admittedly, she thought, he had an air of authority about him, and when she first got to know him she had the utmost respect for him. He was suave and sophisticated, sported a neat little goatee beard and was quite a sharp dresser for his age. He had a knack of saying all the right things, especially to the ladies. Her mother remembered him well as a bit of a catch, back in the day. He had certainly never been short of attention from her friends, casting his charms about as though they were gold dust.

"You will be perfect," he had purred to her, on one of his rare visits to the village shop. "We need people like you to join us!" he continued, making her feel important once more, fool that she was. Only later did she find out from a disgusted Jim, parish councillor of many years standing, that Robin had felt the committee needed to be "prettied up, so we menfolk have something to look at! We might even get some cake!" and by all accounts he had found his own wit highly amusing. Jane shook her head crossly at the thought of it.

"Jane, my dear, have you something you wish to add?"

"Nothing, Chair, nothing at all." His much sharper tones had awakened her from her thoughts with a stab of fear in her chest. That was it, everyone feared him. That was why he had so much power. Jane cast a disinterested glance at item seven. Soon be over. Yes, soon be over.

Her first few meetings had been without any incident whatsoever, and he had been charm itself. He was always at pains to make sure she was included in the discussions, always asked her opinion: "You mums do the finest job in the world. Your opinions matter *so* much to the rest of us, don't you agree?" and the rest of the committee had nodded their dumb assent. But after a while Jane began to notice a pattern. Anything he was in favour of had the shortest amount of discussion time before he deftly moved things along. Especially if anyone showed any signs of dissent. He had courted the attentions of all the ladies on the committee, paying particular attention to Miss Sparrow. True to her name, she twittered around him, fluttering what was left of her ancient eyelashes and mustering her beaky mouth into a wrinkled pout which only served to accentuate her badly drawn lips. His flirtation had, of course, worked, and she agreed with everything that came out of his mouth, nodding so vigorously that Jane thought she was pecking at corn. The same had happened with Mrs Deakin, whom he had invited to join the committee following the untimely death of her husband. Robin had stalked her and then pounced, like a cat with a mouse, and in her grief she had mistaken his attention for kindness. Only when she had disagreed with him at a meeting about one of his projects did she realise his motives, affirmed by the letter he sent to her accusing her of bullying him after all he had done for her in her hour of need. She had never returned to the parish council, such was her state of distress, and he made a start on his next victim to fill her vacancy. His letters were, it turned out, legendary in the village, always accusatory and often defamatory, but no-one dared to stand up to him. Robin's preferred young brunette was naturally poor Mrs Deakin's replacement, and he was the first to congratulate her with an arm around her shoulders and what looked like a whispered compliment in her ear.

"And that, I think, decides *that*," his oily voice oozed out the words bringing item seven to its premature death. Should have paid more attention, thought Jane, as she looked at the brunette's empty chair. Jane doodled again, this time on the back of her agenda, a caricature of RJ with horns and a tail. Robin by name, Robin by nature; he even had a red jumper on tonight.

Lovely to look at, aggressive and bullying to his fellow birds. Fellow men. Jane drew him a beak and a red breast for good measure, and wished she had taken the advice of her art teacher instead of betraying her and defecting to the sciences. Still, the pay was much better in pharmacy, mused Jane as she shaded in the hooded, glinting eyes of her cartoon creation, bringing them scarily close to the real thing.

"And I think that concludes this evening's meeting. Thank you *so* much everyone. And may I say how marvellous it has been to have Jane's witty, insightful company all these years. Tonight I'm afraid we have to say goodbye to you, my dear. We are all *so* sorry to lose you!" and Jane thought that his smile was the only genuine one she had ever seen on his face, probably because he wouldn't have to face any more of her awkward questions. He had never been afraid to show his dislike for Jane, ever since that awful business of the Diamond Jubilee playpark he'd wanted, the 'Robin James Jubilee Playpark', if you please. Jane had led a concerted revolt against the outrageously expensive idea, in a terrible, ill-thought-out location allowing no access for prams and pushchairs or even for the disabled mum who would never have got her motorised wheelchair in there. The plans were shelved, after much acrimony, and ultimately at great cost to the Chairman himself. That would teach him to have expensive plans drawn up without asking anyone.

Sadly, though, Jane reaped the benefit in the form of cold shoulders throughout the village for her and her husband, and even her children. Piano lessons were suddenly booked up; Ladies Circle became more of a square with members huddled in corners and Jane left in the middle; and her husband was dropped from both the darts and the quoits team.

"Thank you, Mr. Chairman, the pleasure has been all mine," (she could purr with the best of them), "and I wonder if you will allow me to serve up a little treat!" Jane disappeared into the kitchen to fetch a tray of butterfly cakes she had made earlier in the day. One of them stood out from all the others, by its sheer size and beauty. This one had jam as well as buttercream icing beneath the delicate sponge wings, and an added special ingredient. She carried the cakes ceremoniously into the hall where the meeting was fragmenting as people prepared to leave. A collective, appreciative, "Aaaaah!" went up as she entered. Robin was effusive, if a little ingenuous, in his praise.

"Oh you are so talented my dear! *So* talented! And you with such a busy life, too!"

You know nothing about my life, she thought as she smiled and graciously took the praise, and serve you right for being so shallow and fatuous as to imagine I was just a pretty face. Jane smiled her sweetest smile as she handed the grandest cupcake to Robin James, who feasted his greedy eyes on the treat. Jane could swear he was salivating.

"I made this especially for you, Robin, in recognition of everything you have done in the past!" He positively glowed as she said this, imagining his effect on the ladies was still intact after all these years and puffing out his important chest as he received the recognition he thought he richly deserved.

"Thank you so much Jane, dear, you are very kind," and Robin James bit into the cupcake. Delicious icing flecked his beard as he licked and laughed his way rapaciously through it. He turned to Jane, wiping the last few entangled crumbs into his handkerchief, saying "I'm afraid I must dash now, my dear, I do hope you will forgive me. All the best!" and he did indeed dash off, as he always did, to avoid any post-meeting discussion which might chip away at his authority.

Jane did not tell him about her secret ingredient. He would find out soon enough, when his chest began to tighten...

Camelot

Paul Wootten

It was a late October afternoon, when the azure sky was laced with milk-white clouds, and loud on the air was the cry of birds. The sun, still fighting for its summer eminence, forced its piercing rays to bathe the land in glory.

"Now, wrap up, mind!"

Peter could never understand this grown-up obsession with buttoned coats and heavy scarves. Only a few weeks ago it had been:

"Come on! Take that shirt off and get some sun on that pale body of yours."

But he had learned that the quickest way to get out to play was to do as they said. An argument only wasted time and they would win anyway. Buttoning up his heavy coat and grabbing his scarf from the peg by the door, he shouted, "See you!" and ran down the path to the lane.

To the left lay all of Oakdene: church, post office, school and the straggling rows of houses that made up the village. Peter turned right. It was half a mile to Michael's house and he had to cross Aspen Copse, an area of tangled scrub that climbed up both sides of the lane, at a point where the land dipped, sending the roadway down into what seemed to Peter to be a tunnel of darkness.

He liked Aspen Copse. Many great games were played here by the village children. It was here that a lot of his real education had taken place. Not the booky kind that came from the small, stone-built school at the heart of the village, with Mrs Drixel and her algebra, but the education about the world and his place in it. It was here that he had fought in the great battles of King Arthur; here he had followed Robin Hood. He learned compassion from victory and honour from defeat. It was here too that he had talked to owls and watched the speckle-sided deer rub its antlers against a tree.

Aspen Copse was amazing this afternoon. The yellow sunlight streamed in angled shafts through the dappled darkness, turning hollows, which hid pretty fungi, into magic theatres where, at any moment, one might see elves at play among the heather and fallen leaves.

*

Michael had a cold. Peter was allowed to stay to watch a video, but kept his distance on the far side of the lounge. Michael's mother let them choose a film from the little, rotating carousel in the corner of the room.

"Are you sure you want to watch this one?" she asked. It was a ghostly thing about werewolves and evil spirits.

"Oh yes! It's cool!" said Peter and Michael together.

By the time the film had finished, the sun had

dipped, exhausted, behind the tree line, and summer had gone.

"I'd better go now, Mrs Parsons." Peter thanked her, waved to Michael and set off for home.

The air was cold, and the tunnel of trees in Aspen Copse looked black and forbidding. Pulling his scarf more tightly round him, Peter put his chin down and walked on quickly, trying to put out of his mind the pictures from that horrible video. The shafts of light had gone. The hollows, stages for the magic show that afternoon, lay cold and empty. The actors had taken their tinsel and brightly coloured props with them, leaving only black screens of menace to hold the clawing images from Peter's own imagination; pictures far worse than those he had seen with Michael.

He hurried on. Suddenly the ragged curtain of darkness was ripped by a sound so terrifying it came to Peter like a piercing beam of light. His body froze, his legs unable to move, his mouth dry, his mind shot through with lights, his senses so alert they penetrated all the shadows for him to find the cause; and yet he did not want to find the cause. He wanted to run. If his legs had let him, that is exactly what he would have done - run and run to the safety of his own front door. But he stood there, frozen by fear.

'Don't be stupid!' he kept telling himself. 'There's nothing to be afraid of, here of all places.'

After all, was this not Sherwood for his Robin? This was a place of refuge not of fear. It was his playground, where he had walked the lanes and run the woods all his life.

"The only thing you need fear is *man*," his father had told him so often before. "Nothing you find in the woods will hurt you, except *man*."

The noise, when it came again, was definitely not human. It was the cry of an animal. Not an animal hunting - Peter knew that cry, having listened often to the owls and heard the midnight fox - but an animal afraid. He knew that if he ran now he would hate himself forever, for turning his back on a creature in distress. What would Sir Launcelot do? There was no need to think further, for Aspen Copse was already turning into the forest around Camelot, and he, Sir Peter, had left the lane and was climbing the steep bank, into the wood. His own fear melted now that there was something real to do. He listened for the cry to come again.

It was a strange cry, strident and hissing, a mixture of anger, frustration and fear, and before Peter reached it he knew what it was. It was the cry of a cat.

It was a small black cat, with a great flue-brush of a tail and large, staring eyes. Around its neck a blue collar with a bell had been fitted by some caring owner hoping to control the flea population. The collar was caught in a twist of wire that hung broken from a fence post. As the cat struggled, the wire moved with it, jagging its neck with its cruel barbs.

Slipping his coat off, Peter placed it carefully around the cat, so as to lock its claws inside a duffel cocoon, while he worked on the collar.

Cats can bite and scratch, none worse than frightened cats. So Peter, speaking gently all the time and watching out for sharp teeth, steadily unbuckled the collar.

There was blood all around the creature's neck, but the collar came away easily and, to Peter's relief, the cat was purring. Keeping it wrapped in his coat he walked on home.

His mother helped to bathe the wound, while he held on tightly to his purring bundle.

"It must belong to someone in the village," she was saying. "They will be worried about it. Look, Peter, it's only a tiny wound." She parted the hair for him to see where the grey flesh stood livid beneath the torn fur. "This should heal quickly."

There was no address on the collar, so they gave the cat a saucer of milk and decided to try to find its owner in the morning. That night it slipped quietly on to the end of Peter's bed, looked at him for a moment with its big, green eyes, curled its long brush of a tail around itself and fell asleep.

*

"Do we *have to* find its owner, Mum?" Peter asked at breakfast. "It seems ever so happy here, look." The cat had followed him downstairs, used the box of rich earth his father had organized hurriedly before they went to bed, eaten half a tin of pilchards opened especially for it, and now lay on a cushion, watching Peter, its eyes half-closed in a rumbling purr of contentment.

"Of course we must, dear. How would you feel if it was your cat that was lost? Anyway, I'm sure he'll be glad to get home."

*

It was Peter who was glad to get home the next afternoon. School had been fine: he always liked Monday because they had PE in the morning and art in the afternoon. PE was his favourite lesson, maybe because he was good at it. He could climb the ropes and watch everyone else running about the hall like the little people from the story of Gulliver's Travels which his aunt had just bought for him. He loved the picture of the giant, Gulliver, looking around him at the tiny Lilliputians rushing about his feet in terror. He imagined, just for a moment that he was the giant and he had complete control over everyone beneath him.

"Come down now, Peter," Mrs Drixel called up to him. "You must give someone else a turn."

"Oh, Miss," he complained taking one last look around. But he knew better than to argue with her.

In the art lesson that afternoon he painted a picture of a cat, a small black cat with an enormous, fluffy tail, and when it was time to go home he quickly grabbed his coat and rushed out of the school.

The small black cat was waiting for him, curled up on a chair in the front room. It stood up, arched its back and stretched itself, then jumped down to rub its glossy fur on Peter's leg.

"Hey Mum, listen, he's purring. I think he likes me." Peter reached down and stroked the black fur. The cat pushed its face up towards Peter so that he could fondle its ears. He found the patch of rough fur where the cruel wire had cut into the flesh. There was a crusty scab there, but the cat didn't pull away, it just stood gazing up at Peter with its huge green eyes.

*

That night, when Peter was in bed, he felt a soft thump on his feet as the small black bundle of fur settled itself down for the night and curled up, pressing itself into him. In the morning it was still there, warm and contented on the foot of his bed.

*

The next evening, when Peter returned home from school, his mum announced that she had made enquiries at the post office and had succeeded in finding the cat's owners. Peter's eyes filled with tears as he sank his fingers into the soft, black fur and rubbed his chin in the back of the purring animal's neck. 'Life is not fair!' he thought. It was obvious that the cat liked him. It purred and purred, opening and closing its claws on Peter's knee.

They took the cat back to its owners, a herdsman and his wife, who lived in a cottage on the edge of Aspen Copse.

Peter's bed seemed strangely empty that night. He missed those big, green eyes and that tail looking so out of place on a smooth, black cat.

*

Peter still goes to Aspen Copse, quite often, and the battles of Robin Hood or King Arthur are fought over and over again, beneath the patient branches of the trees. But, if you were to watch really closely, you would see a new friend amongst the gallant band of warriors, a friend who climbs the trees better than all the others, and watches Peter wherever he goes. He carries his own banner with him: a jet black plume of honour, love and loyalty that flies once more in Camelot.

Switching Hearts

Tamsyn Naylor

As I looked down at him quietly sleeping, his long gentle breaths rose and fell in his chest like warm, welcoming waves of life washing onto the shore. He was contented and at one; nothing could disturb his rest. I had a lot to thank this gentle, thoughtful man for: he had loved me for many years and was always the warm beating heart of the home when I returned in the evening.

How could I have put that out of my mind? How could I shut my ordinary home life in a box and think it was right to do some of the things I had foolishly thought important and vibrant amongst my newly found, so-called friends? I really had been living a bit of a dream, thinking I was stuck in a rut and needing to change things. There was nothing wrong with my life as it was really, just silly niggly things.

It had started with a feeling of not really mattering; not particularly *me* not mattering, but more, *things*. What did it matter if the pots were left in the sink for another time and still came to be there three days later? Why care if the tiles in the shower had come loose, if we were just careful with the water for a while until he could get round to fixing it, all in good time? But that was the

70

problem: it became that all those things which had not mattered before, did, and this had unsettled me.

Getting out and about with work colleagues had made a nice change: I chatted with them and laughed over silly anecdotes. It was nice to fit in amongst others after spending time on my own, with no-one but the kids to talk to. But now it was just us and I found the glimpses into other people's lives over a pleasant drink quite refreshing. Of course, the time I wasn't at home myself reflected in the house: a few neglected bits and pieces soon accumulated. It would be quite a task to make our home presentable again, and as for the garden, well, at least nettles are good for the butterflies.

Well, I had let things slip and, of course, lost sight of what really mattered, but then so had he. As he fidgeted slightly, his weight caused the bed to creak and groan in complaint. He had patiently accepted I would not be in much this week, but he had not put that time to good use in my absence. I looked down at the crumpled sheets and could see my book teetering on the edge of the bed as if undecided whether to fall and wake him, or wait to be read. A few moments ago I had crept in, navigated the footboard and reached to turn the bedside light on, with a view to finishing the chapter before bedtime, but the wires had sparked and flashed. Even my body hitting the floor had not woken him, and now I was gazing down at my own lifeless form which lay there, sprawled awkwardly along the side of the bed. How many times had I mentioned that the plug was loose? Each time I pulled my hairdryer out after use, the screws would rattle and squirm. Now the room was silent and dark, apart from the whispered sighs from his slumbering form.

I had so many regrets, so many things I wanted to say to him. I didn't care for the unfinished jobs now but there was so much more left to do. I silently wept and tried to reach out but the room filled with a new bright light and he seemed so distant that I couldn't reach him.

First Love

John Watson

I draw the curtains back in my small bedroom and stare out at the leaden grey sky of the morning. It does nothing to brighten my mood and as I rub the sleep from my eyes, I hear mother calling for me to hurry as she hates the embarrassment of walking into church late. Dressing hurriedly, I arrive for breakfast and grab a slice of toast before everything is whisked away and another boring day stretches ahead of me.

Grabbing me by the collar, my mother ushers me out of the door and I submissively traipse behind my elders like an obedient dog. On arrival, I slip inside and become one of the many, anonymous now, in this dark and sombre world they call the House of God.

I sit alongside my parents, sullen, silent, my mind drifting back to when I so loved and admired them. Everything we did back then, we did together. The games, the laughter, the holidays we shared. What happened? Why have they changed into such priggish, boring people? All their false talk and fixed smiles make me feel like throwing up. Mother always was prim and proper, but Father and I used to share jokes, laugh with each other, play games and enjoy life. Now, here he is, stern faced and sitting ramrod straight to my right, never a muscle twitching. I hear the preacher begin his sermon and I drift off into my own private world, wondering how many of these apparently upright and steadfast people really are God-fearing and how many attend just for appearance's sake?

Suddenly, the preacher man stuns me back to reality, thumping the massive oak pulpit with his fist, his sermon reaching its fire and brimstone peak on the depravity of the human race. I tremble at the sheer ferocity of the man as he launches into his attack on the sins of the flesh. Spittle flies from his mouth. Beads of perspiration appear on his brow, such is the intensity of his sermon. But, just as suddenly, he becomes gentle as he quietly leads the congregation into prayer.

I lower my head with the rest of the congregation and take the chance to steal a furtive glance across the aisle and notice a blonde-haired girl about my age sitting slightly behind me. I begin to wonder if she has come because of her parents, like me. She is slightly built; her black jumper and skirt stand out as sombre, a complete contrast to her golden hair which is drawn back into a pony tail. Her eyes are closed, head bowed, clutching a small bible, her lips moving in silent prayer, but suddenly, maybe feeling my eyes upon her, she lifts her head and smiles. I feel my cheeks burst crimson and I hurriedly look away. I bury my head in the hymn book and the next time I steel myself to try and catch her eye, she has gone. Quietly, silently, she has left the church and I wonder if I will ever see her again.

After lunch I return to my bedroom. Guilt sweeps over me as I sneak the magazines from their hiding place to gaze at the pictures of illicit beauty.

My mood darkens with frustration and uncertainty. Are these thoughts immoral? Is this what the preacher man means? Surely not. This is only my weird and wonderful fantasy world. A lonely world I fall toward constantly. The emptiness draws me forward into the slough of depressing darkness that I feel I may never come out of.

I squeeze my eyes tight shut to stop the tears. So tight, it hurts. I hear the preacher again. See him, perched high in his pulpit, his words echoing around my brain: "Read the good book. Do not be drawn toward the path of decadence and depravity. It can only lead to destruction. There will be no salvation for the weak and they will be committed to the burning fires of Hell for all eternity."

Surely, I will never enter the Kingdom of God now!

I open my eyes. My bedroom is frighteningly silent. Silent as a tomb. Nothing has changed.

Tidying my room, I rush out, calling to my mother that I will be back before dark.

Lonely, head low, I trudge the street in a state of

despondency, and then I hear a voice calling. As I look up, my heart jumps slightly. I see the girl from church. I mumble a greeting and she crosses over to walk alongside, introducing herself as Claire, saying she has just moved into the avenue a couple of weeks ago.

"Can I walk with you for a while, seeing that we both appear to be going the same way?" she asks. I notice the start of a quirky smile, the smile she gave me in church when she caught me staring. I blush again at the thought, replying that she can walk with me, but that I'm not really in a talkative mood.

"That's okay," she says, "I'll do the talking," and she begins to chatter incessantly. After a few moments my mood brightens and I begin to enjoy her company, her natural friendliness and warmth.

As we pass the cinema, Claire casually asks if I have seen the latest film that's showing.

"No," I reply. Then, taking a deep breath, I bravely ask, "Would you like to see it?"

"I would love too, but I have never had anyone to go with. Until now, that is." Her huge smile and the sparkling blue eyes that hold mine for just a split second longer than necessary lift the final clouds of despair from me as we enter this other, different, but acceptable, fantasy world together. I feel excited, elated, and keep glancing across at this beautiful girl sitting next to me. I cannot believe this is happening. She must like me or she wouldn't have come to the film with me, would she?

These insecure thoughts race through my brain in wicked confusion as I once again cast furtive glances at her. Her long blonde hair, now loose, tumbles to her shoulders. I notice the soft paleness of her skin, the slight upturn of her nose, the sparkle of her eyes staring intently at the drama unfolding on screen. I study her every move, her mannerisms, her laugh, her total naturalness. My skin begins to prickle. I feel excitement ripple through my whole body as for the first time in years, I feel alive.

After the film we sit and talk, totally absorbed in our own little world. Suddenly we look around and everyone has gone, the huge cinema silent. We stand up to go. Should I kiss her now, or should I wait? I stand awkwardly, uncertainty making me clam up. I touch her shoulder and she turns and tilts her head slightly to look at me. Then reaching up she pulls my head down to hers and I feel the warmth of her breath on my cheek before our lips touch and we kiss. A long, lingering kiss that sends shock waves through my body leaving me stunned. I turn and follow her dazedly outside.

Gathering my thoughts, I ask, "Are you doing anything tomorrow?"

"Nothing that I can't change," she replies.

"Could we maybe meet up tomorrow then?"

"Would you like to?" she asks.

"Yes," I reply eagerly, and I feel myself grinning

from ear to ear.

"Oh, that's good. I would have been disappointed if you hadn't wanted to."

We wave goodbye and somehow the huge grin on my face appears to be fixed in place. I have never felt so happy, never felt such sheer joy surge through my whole being, my mind constantly returning to her. Especially the kiss. That bombshell of a kiss. My legs go weak thinking about it.

On returning home, I enter the kitchen where mother and father are sitting. I join them at the table.

"Cup of tea, son?" Mam asks.

"Love one, thanks."

Dad's reading the sports page. "Picked any winners lately, Dad, or are they still racing donkeys off the beach?" This was one of his favourite sayings when he lost, which he mostly did.

He pokes his head over the top of the page and a wry smile that I hadn't noticed of late breaks the stern look. "I've just spotted one as you came in the room, son. This could be a good one to have a couple of bob on."

"Oh, what's it called?"

"Young Romancer. Just a beginner like, but it should have a good chance as long as it's a stayer." He looks directly at me and a wide grin splits his features. We both crack up laughing until tears are streaming down our faces.

"See, I told you Doris," Dad says, "he hasn't had the operation for a sense of humour bypass. It's what they call growing up."

I leave them to their cup of tea and wonder how it was possible for my parents to change in such a short space of time. Shaking my head in disbelief, I climb the stairs to my room expecting the all-engulfing gloom and emotional turmoil to descend. But the storm is over. My thoughts are now on the future as I drift off into a relaxed sleep, to dream of Claire.

Waking early, I pull the curtains back. The sun blazes through, bathing it in light, a haven of peace once again. In a matter of hours, an injection of enthusiasm for life has suddenly transformed me. The boring mediocrity that seemed to stretch before me is now one of expectancy as I have a friend who I feel I can share many things with.

Free from guilt, free from the shackles of loneliness that restrained me, I am so looking forward to seeing Claire again.

Retribution

Ray Stewart

Alan carried out his final checks on the boat. Mooring lamps lit, hawsers secure, with enough slack to allow for the rise and fall of the tide. That'll do her, he thought and, stepping ashore, he headed for The Angel.

As he walked along the quayside he glanced back at the boat. His 'breadwinner' he called it, although the name over the stern read 'Janie W', and the letters at her prow WY607. He turned right, heading away from the waterfront and climbed the steep bank heading for his favourite pub. A pint or two of Jennings would slake his thirst and help him to sleep better tonight.

Entering the Angel, he smiled at Gilly, the barmaid. A possibility, he thought. He was reaching his forty-fifth year, but he reckoned he was still worthy of his reputation. He had always had an eye for the girls. His friends used to joke about him having a girl in every port, and in this case it was almost true. A girl in North Shields had 'entertained' him on one of his layovers, and there was always a girl or three he could call upon when he was in Yarmouth.

He sat with his pint near the window in the small room, and reflected on his life with some satisfaction. He had first gone to sea as a sixteen year old deckhand on that battered, weather-beaten trawler that belonged to Old John. He had served his apprenticeship there. He had endured the hard seas and the hard life for some five or six years before joining one of the bigger ocean-going boats from Whitby. It was only a temporary berth of course. He had been ambitious, scrimping and saving every penny that he could. He was not the sort of man to spend his life as a wage slave working for others. Alan had always wanted to be his own boss.

And so at the ripe old age of twenty-six, he had scraped enough together to buy an old tub, The Charlotte Grey. Sailing as her master and owner, he soon reaped the profits from the sea.

He had met a girl of course, and married her shortly after she had announced that he was going to be a father. He even, in a romantic moment, renamed the boat after her, the Charlotte Grey becoming the Carol B. If his life had continued in this vein then perhaps things would have been better now. He was certainly good as a trawler man and before long the Carol B was traded in for a newer and bigger boat, imaginatively called the Carol B II. On the waterfront at Whitby, he looked the respectable boat owner and master, with a wife and two children. But then his wandering eye took over. He had the odd fling here and the odd adventure there, usually when he was away from home, and of course, what Carol didn't know couldn't hurt her.

That was until he met Janie. How long ago was that? Must be nearly twelve years ago now. She was different from the others. For a start, it was the nearest thing to love that he had ever experienced. He was fond of Carol of course, but... there was something special about Janie. Like him, she was also married.

They had met in the Angel one summer's evening. They were cautious in the beginning, with the pretensions of a platonic relationship. Then one evening, after the drink had removed the caution – and their inhibitions – the relationship become a little more heated. That first evening they had gone down to the moonlit beach and made frantic love on the sand. They met and 'loved' in secret, but this was not enough. They both decided that they wanted to be together on a more permanent basis. They planned to leave their respective partners and move away from Whitby where they could begin a new life. They planned to tell their partners on the same day and the date was agreed. Then, with their bags packed, they would sail on the Carol B to another port where they could rent a berth onshore whilst looking for something more permanent. Alan remembered that the date agreed was just over ten years ago.

Alan had had his bags packed and already stowed on the boat. He'd gone home to tell Carol of his intentions, but when he saw her, she was in a state of excitement. "You're going to be a daddy again!" she blurted out. Alan was stunned. This was not the time to tell her that he was leaving her. He went through the pretence of being happy, hugging and kissing his wife.

After an hour or so he'd made the excuse of having to go to check up on the boat and left for the quayside. He'd found Janie sitting expectantly in the wheelhouse. He broke the news to her as gently as he could; that their life together would have to be put on hold. In her desperation, and tears, Janie told him to forget about it. She had always known in her heart that he wouldn't have the courage to go through with it. She would return to her husband with her tail between her legs and beg forgiveness. It was over between them. She stepped off the boat into the darkness and they went their separate ways.

He'd heard later that her husband, instead of being pleased at her return had beaten her, and then, throwing her onto the floor of the kitchen, had raped her. Left alone after the assault, she opened the back door and disappeared into the night.

Her clothes had been found later, stacked neatly in a pile, near to the spot on the beach at Sandsend, where she and Alan had first made love. Footsteps led to the water's edge, but of Janie there was not a trace. "Now when was that?" he thought. "May the thirty-first. Must be ten years ago." The thought came to his head that it must be near the thirty-first today. He always lost track of the days when he had been at sea. Looking across at Gilly he asked, "What's the date today?"

"The thirty-first, my love," she replied. "New month tomorrow."

"A double Talisker," he said, and Gilly obligingly handed him a large measure of his favourite whiskey. He took it back to his seat, raised it, and whispered the toast, "Janie." Looking through his glass he noticed a slim figure enter the room. He put the glass down and stared at the girl in front of him.

"It can't be you. You're..."

"Dead," she finished his sentence for him. "How about merely disappeared? You saw that film with me where Sergeant Troy faked his own death, didn't you?"

"Yes of course," he said meekly. Then looking at her face, "You're still as beautiful as you were on the last day that I saw you. You don't look a day older."

"Well I am," she replied. "Can't say that time has been as kind to you though," and she sat down on the chair opposite him. Shaking, he went to the bar, returning with a glass of gin which he placed in front of her.

"You remember," she smiled before they began to engage in small talk, the kind that recently-reunited people who are a little uncomfortable in each other's company indulge in.

There was only the one serious question that she asked him. "Are you with anyone?" she said.

"No. I'm on my own," he replied. "After your disappearance there were rumours, and they reached Carol's ears. She challenged me and I couldn't lie to her. I told her that I loved someone else, and that someone else was you. She left me, taking the kids with her." At the sound of the word 'loved' Janie had raised her eyebrows slightly... And then the conversation returned to the trivia.

How long they sat there, Alan did not know, but when they left arm in arm, the table was littered with empty glasses. They walked through the darkened streets of Whitby, reaching the steps leading to the beach.

"Where are we going?" he asked.

"Where we can be alone together," she said, and, taking his hand, she led him down the steps to the beach, and the waiting tide.

Jack Frost

Paul Wootten

The cobbled streets were thick with ice; horses slipped awkwardly, jangling the leather and brass harness and rocking the carts. The carters sat behind, wrapped up tight with woollen mufflers around their necks and faces. Thick leather gloves held the traces which in turn were stiffened with the cold. One carter, William Main, left the town behind, and started out on the country lane to Bamford. He was older than most and used to these winter mornings. He coaxed his horse along with little clicking sounds which rang strangely in the dry air. Icicles hung from the low branches of the trees beside the road, but they had formed days ago. There was no sign of a thaw just yet. And then the snow started. It fell silently: little, fluffy, feather-like pieces of purest white drifted relentlessly down to settle on everything they touched. It settled on the road; it settled on the rooftops; it settled on the tops of gate-posts, and it settled on William Main. Tiny flecks of white tickled his eye-lashes, making him blink and screw up his eyes. Cold drips fell from his crumpled hat to trickle down his neck. He glanced behind at his packages, neatly stacked in the cart. They, too, were quickly being lost beneath the soft covering of snow. The lane, the ditch and the verge were fast becoming one, and the old horse had noticeably slowed his pace as he picked his way along.

"It's alright, old boy," William said, the steam of his breath rising and dancing with the falling flakes. "Keep your eyes on the road. The White Hart's only round the corner. I think we'll stop there for a bit."

He was not the only carter to stop at the White Hart that morning. As he entered the snug he heard voices welcoming him in, but it took a moment for his old eyes to accommodate to the smoky darkness. He felt the glorious warmth of the fire which raged against the cold, hissing and spitting the damp from the logs. He slumped down in a chair, shook the snow from his old hat, and warmed his feet against the blaze. The barman brought him a tankard of foaming ale as his friends pulled their chairs nearer.

"This is a bit of a do, William," Daniel Bright began. "I'll have a job getting to Garford today in this."

"If this goes on I think we'll all be stuck here for the night," William sighed. "Blasted Jack Frost! He does this sometime every year, and every year we lose money through him." He flexed his toes in the toasty warmth of his steaming boots, undid his coat, sipped his ale and silently prayed that the snow would last all day.

Thunderstruck

Elizabeth Smith

The night had been stifling. Even with the bedroom window wide open there had not been the slightest hint of a breeze, and now that the sun had risen the heat was building. Kate sighed, that early morning cool shower had only provided a small respite from this hot muggy weather. "God, I hope it breaks soon," she muttered. She got out of bed, aware of the furry lump sprawled out in the middle of the duvet. Samson, her lovely red tabby cat, was oblivious to all around him. As Kate gently stroked him he purred and licked her hand. It must be nice to be a cat, she thought.

Kate opened her wardrobe door and, after some sorting through her clothes, she found a loose-fitting skirt and blouse. The view in the long mirror reminded her of the time she and hubby were in Egypt in August when the daytime temperature was 35 degrees in the shade; now *that* was hot.

Kate smiled and turned to go down stairs. Her husband was watching the news. Like her, he didn't like the hot weather and had spent a fitful night. "I maybe late home," he said. "I'll phone and let you know what I am doing," and with his usual kiss, he left.

Kate busied herself with making some fresh tea. She left the back door open and went into the sitting room and watched the rest of the news. The local weather forecast showed the hot weather was set to continue with possible isolated thunderstorms. Great.

She went back into the kitchen and poured herself another mug of tea. She stepped outside. The heat hit her like a sledge hammer. She stood and listened. In the distance she could hear the drone of the traffic and the incessant hum of the steel works; what she could not hear were the birds chattering to each other. Strange, she thought.

Glancing up at the sky, she remembered that yesterday at this time it had been a really deep, cloudless blue, but now it took on the appearance of polished metal, and clouds were bubbling on the horizon. She could still feel the heat from the blazing sun, and decided to go inside.

Back inside, she washed the pots and went upstairs to make the bed. Samson was still on it, the tip of his tail twitching. Kate tickled his chin and he opened his eyes, but there seemed to be a hint of fear in them. Despite the warmth in the room, Kate suddenly felt cold. She shook herself. The bed could wait. She began to sort out the laundry instead. With the washer running, she went back into the garden and inspected her tomato plants which really needed watering, but in this strong sunlight they too would have to wait.

Later, in the kitchen, most of her morning's chores completed, Kate turned on the fan and rejoiced in the cool air that it emitted. She put the TV on and went to make her lunch. She had just shut the fridge when Samson appeared. He didn't purr like he would normally do, demanding food. Instead he went to the back door and looked out.

Samson sniffed the air, his tail moving in an agitated manner.

"What's the matter, puss?" Kate said, stroking him. Samson let out a noise that was neither a purr or a growl, turned and looked at Kate. Once again, Kate felt cold. She took her lunch into the room and ate it half-heartedly. The local weather forecast now showed downpours, localised flooding and possible electrical disruptions. Bloody hell, thought Kate. Perhaps Samson could sense a huge storm coming.

She went into the kitchen and, as she did so, she heard a long, distant rumble of thunder. Best close the back door, she thought, remembering the last thunder storm when the kitchen floor was awash with rainwater. Feeling tired now, she settled herself down on the settee to watch her favourite sitcom, aware that Samson had jumped up and snuggled down beside her.

She must have dropped off because the next thing she saw was a blinding flash of lightning that was followed immediately by a deafening clap of thunder. Kate jumped up. The room was practically dark and the TV was dead. She tried the lights −nothing, in fact all the electrics were off. Kate was rather frightened. Another brilliant flash of lightning filled the room followed by a massive booming noise which seem to shake the whole house and outside the rain was coming down like stair-rods. Samson was still on the settee, but he was wide awake and making low mewing noises . She picked him up and cuddled him.

Kate now felt distinctly unsettled. She went to the window and looked out. The street was awash with rainwater which was now running down the drive, no doubt into the garden. She was also aware of at least two house alarms going off.

She glanced at the clock: it was getting on for dinnertime. She'd be able to peel some potatoes and get the salad ready, but she would not be able to make the quiche until the power came back on.

Kate went upstairs and looked out of the back bedroom window. The sky was still a sombre grey but the rain seemed to be easing. There was another flash of lightning followed by a crash of thunder. Just for a moment, Kate wished she was back in Egypt enjoying the warmth of the sun.

She felt she needed the loo, probably just a nervous reaction but she went any way. Then, she madeup the bed. Turning to go downstairs, she was greeted by Samson; like all males, he liked attention. She picked him up. Samson purred and put his front paw on her cheek. "What is the matter, puss?" He still seemed agitated. They went down stairs.

At the bottom of the stairs she picked the phone up and felt reassured when she heard the dialling tone. In fact, she almost wished it would ring.

Kate was at loss now what to do. She didn't like this feeling. Then, as if by magic, the house came to life. The fridge began to hum. Kate turned the oven on and the fan burst into life. She turned it off. Excellent, everything was returning to normal. She went into the living room and spotted the two letters. God, those really needed posting. Kate glanced at the clock and opened the backdoor. The storm was easing. A quick walk to the letterbox seemed like a good idea. She put on her waterproofs and stepped outside. As she turned to lock the door, Samson stood looking out at the soggy garden. She motioned him to go out and perhaps pay a call of nature, but Samson was having none of it He turned and went to his litter tray. Kate locked the door and set off to the letterbox.

It was still raining and there was a lot of surface water running down the road. Just then, out of the blue, a car flashed past her at a ridiculous speed and what seemed like a huge wave of water hit her, soaking her legs and lower back. Kate gasped. "Effing idiot!" Kate shouted. Where was a police car when you wanted one? She half ran the rest of the way. On reaching the letter box she shoved the very damp letters through the slot and turned to make her way home. There another roll of thunder which, thankfully, sounded some way off.

As she arrived back home, wet and cold, she glanced up at the roof to see if the storm had dislodged any tiles. Thankfully, everything seemed to be intact. In the front bedroom window she spotted Samson peering out. She smiled. Poor Samson. Perhaps now he will calm down. Kate unlocked the back door and stepped onto the mat and, in an instant, Samson was at her side. She quickly pulled off her very wet waterproofs and placed them on the kitchen floor. As she turned to shut the door she thought she could hear a bird singing. Kate went upstairs and changed out of her wet clothes, went into the bathroom, rubbed a towel through her hair, brushed it, and then went down stairs. She looked at the clock. Shit! Andrew would be home in half an hour and dinner wasn't ready! Nothing worse than a hungry husband. She turned on the oven and busied herself making the dinner.

Fifteen minutes later the quiche and the potatoes were cooking. Kate went to the sink and washed up the baking stuff, aware that the sun was now shining. Then she realised Andrew hadn't phoned her and once again she felt uneasy. She went into hall and stood looking at the phone. Shall I ring him? she wondered. She was just about to pick up the receiver when she felt Samson weaving around her ankles. He was making that noise again. She picked him up and he instantly dug his claws into her arm. Kate was astounded by this action. He hadn't done this since he was a kitten, when a much larger cat had scared him while he was in the back garden. Kate held him. He was shaking. Just then there was a knock at the front door. Kate slowly opened it. She was greeted by two policewomen.

"Mrs Kate Gallon?" said one of them. Kate nodded. "May we come in?"

"Yes," whispered Kate. The next few minutes were a gut-wrenching nightmare. The words flooded her mind: road, detour, backwash, driving too fast, crash...

A single tear rolled down Kate's cheek like a raindrop down a windowpane and she knew her life would never be the same again.

Fly on the Wall

Tamsyn Naylor

Heady scent emanated from the wilted, droopy rose heads overhanging the garden path. The hot summer afternoon was draining to the point that the woman's temper had built up to waspishness as the hoverflies lingered around her face. All she was doing was taking the deadheads off and she could get no peace. As she swiped her hand past her face for the umpteenth time, a bluebottle clumsily bombed past on its way into the porch.

The house was cool, the tiled floor damp with condensation. The zuzzing fly had flown into the front room and was inspecting every corner, all along the top of the wall, into the alcove where the china ornament of a frilly, pink-cheeked girl stood, and along the curtain pole into the window. Its flight was quite purposeful, its quest to record household items, wallpaper designs, paint schemes, furnishings, whether or not the householder had double glazing or satellite television, collections of DVDs, anything that would let his employer know the tastes of the individual.

The fly continued through the passageway and into the kitchen. Scanning around the room it recorded what cereals and tins were in the cupboard, the make of the oven, the fact there was no bread-maker on the worktop, the age of the dining chairs and the utensils hanging from a swinging hook in the ceiling. There was a lot of potential from an advertiser's viewpoint in this room alone; the victims of this surveillance shoot would have a varied onslaught of advertising leaflets with offers from the local supermarket, kitchens, furniture, vouchers and floor-covering companies. Heading on up the staircase and into the bathroom, the bluebottle covered every area, taking in cleaning products, towelling, bedding and even crossing in front of the medicine cabinet for signs of health food and homeopathic remedies. Little did the lady in the rose bed know what she had in store.

Later that afternoon, the man of the house was pacing up and down the lawn, fastidiously cutting stripes into the grass with the mower. A cluster of flies encircled him, checking out the condition of the mower, noting the soil type of the lawn, what kinds of vegetables he was growing and whether he had any Dutch bulbs in his borders. With these he would be eligible for a free carriage clock. One or two flies were scrutinising the shelves of the shed, lined with various plant food and weed-killing products and assorted tins of 'might come in handy someday' paint. As it was summer, there was a lot of potential to bombard the household TV screens and doormats with invitations to come to the local DIY stores; what better way to spend your holiday? If the findings of the pesky peekers turned up evidence of badly-done household chores, with the thought in mind that if you do a job badly, then 'the missus' will not ask you again, or even worse, scenes of 'I can do that' carnage where things were never finished and were left in a dangerous state, then a profusion of leafleting would follow from local tradesmen and jack-of-alls.

The lawn now resembled the Oxford stripe blouse that his wife had bought with the store card she was recommended to take after becoming a 'Premier Customer.' Locked away in the humble shed, purchased from the 'region's finest summerhouse specialist', the man was now applying 'superior stain and colour, exactly what it says on the tin', to his fence.

The success of the symbiotic relationship between the insects and the advertising spin doctors was a strong one. For years now, masses of pictures, samples and data had been fed back to a central database, which was the powerhouse for producing masses of mailbox shoots, email infiltration and telephone messaging systems. Every part of human activity was monitored with the intention of feeding back the information to potential suppliers. Hoverflies and bluebottles were the cheapest and most extensive ways of 'accessing all areas.' The seemingly insignificant presence of something as unimportant as a fly around humans meant that the true purpose was masked. The technology of the surveillance equipment needed to be hugely advanced to cope with demand; charging points were provided at the copious brown docking stations situated in fields and parks, wherever cattle were to be found. Very brief stops were all that was needed to power up the devices.

But what could stop the progress of these hungry companies? How could the huge volume of data recording be curtailed and the hopeless waste of unwanted material stopped? By man's greatest ally: the spider. Since time immemorial, the much maligned spider had been targeting flies, and now the data-flies provided many a juicy meal. Little do we know that when we overlook the presence of spiders in our houses and garden rooms, they are actually working for the benefit of man.

At a chaotically busy city office, early one morning, the cleaners were busy sweeping round and dusting. The long-tickler was scouring the corners of the room, taking down dust and cobwebs from the boardroom walls. An hour from now a highly charged meeting was to be held, deciding on the future of the company. Through the glass screen, the minions at their desks were spilling rumours as to the new spider-resistant spy-bot soon to be unveiled – a bee, perhaps? Or a wasp? – and what this development would mean to them. A rather suspicious employee said to his fellow workmate, "I wish I could be a fly on the wall in there..."

The Invisible Man

Delphine Gale

The mirror never lies. It can play the odd trick or two on you from time to time, but it never lies. Stewart Campbell avoided eye contact with himself as he straightened his bow tie in readiness for work. Satisfied at last that he wouldn't fall foul of The Manager's strict dress code, he grabbed his notebook and his jacket, stroked the last invisible hair from it as he shrugged his narrow shoulders into it and ran downstairs and out into the clear, bright dawn. He mustn't be late for his shift.

He ran swiftly and silently up the back steps into the staff entrance of the elegant Georgian hotel where he worked, almost bumping into Malcolm Murray, with whom he was on breakfast duty.

"Steady on, Stewy, almost ran me over there! Are you late? Or just miles away again?!" Malcolm laughed and pushed past Stewart to put the coffee pots on the shelf, ready for the morning's work.

"I think we're almost full. It'll be busy." Stewart's soft voice could hardly be heard over the rattle of the cups and saucers, but Malcolm glanced back over his shoulder and winked theatrically. The two young men were part of the team of butlers employed to pander to the every whim of the guests who graced them with their presence at The Mountfield, a small boutique hotel in the heart of Edinburgh, and which discreetly boasted its five star status in an effort to attract the right kind of guest. The Manager had his doubts about that; it seemed every Tom, Dick and Hooray Henry could afford to stay there these days, he lamented to his staff. Malcolm wasn't complaining: there were some very nice posh hen parties from time to time. He had given many a whisky-laden hen her last taste of freedom, and used, "I'm descended from *the* Stuarts, you know," as a chat up line. It worked, often, not because it was true (it wasn't), but because of his dark good looks, lithe body and mischievous eyes, and his white, even smile that had disarmed many unsuspecting females, of all ages. His mission in life was to set Stewart up with a girl, which seemed to be proving difficult.

Around mid-morning, as the breakfast tables were cleared after the late-risers, and re-laid for afternoon tea (lunch is so passé, The Manager decreed), a rumpus was heard in reception. A man's voice could be heard directing the passage of his luggage, and demanding the young German receptionist be replaced with someone he could understand, for God's sake. The Manager appeared at the dining room door, a little flustered, and waved Stewart to come through.

"Please take this luggage to the Isla suite," he instructed Stewart, taking back control of the situation, "for Sir Clive and Lady Harvey." Stewart nodded, and was about to ask if they would like to take the lift or the stairs when Sir Clive's mobile rang. "Get out of the bloody way, woman!" he roared at his wife, who had committed no greater sin than trying to keep out of his way while he took command of the hotel and booked them in. He wandered out into the hallway, speaking loudly and jovially into his phone as he went, clearly oblivious to anything else around him. Stewart noticed Lady Harvey had retreated to a seat in reception, waiting for her husband to finish, and he quietly asked her if she would like to go up to the room or wait.

"Oh please, let's just get a move on," came her exasperated reply as she cast an annoyed glance in the direction of her guffawing husband, and, taking the lift, Stewart showed her into the room.

"Thank you so much, you are very kind." She threw her fur coat onto the bed.

"Would you like me to unpack for you, ma'am?" Stewart was standing by the door, head slightly bowed, hands behind his back. Malcolm would have joked with her, and she would have joked back no doubt, but Stewart's confidence was already at its peak.

"Thank you, no, but could you please bring up some tea?" Lady Harvey looked in dire need of some refreshment. She smiled gratefully at Stewart and he disappeared to the kitchen.

"Who's that moron?" Malcolm wanted to know,

nodding towards a still chatting Sir Clive. "I'll take the tea up for you, Stewy, I quite liked the look of that Dame," and Malcolm winked to show Stewart it would pointless arguing. Not that he would; Stewart had never been able to argue with anyone. He found it easier to back down.

The following morning Stewart met Sir Clive and Lady Harvey again at breakfast. He was first on duty, and was surprised to see them so early in the dining room. He took their order. Looking first at Lady Harvey, as he was trained to do, he asked what she would like.

"Orange juice, freshly squeezed. And coffee," was her unuttered reply, voiced by her husband. "And I will have apple juice, and a pot of Earl Grey." No 'please', no 'thank you', no manners. Sir Clive cleared his throat and, shaking out a broadsheet, effectively screened himself from further interference. Lady Harvey caught Stewart's eye and mouthed, "With hot milk please." A few minutes later, Stewart returned with the order, stood discreetly back and asked what they would like to eat. Once again Sir Clive barked the order for both of them and returned abruptly to his financial pages, pausing only to wave for more tea and coffee. Lady Harvey lowered her head and waited for her breakfast. Apart from thanking Stewart at the end of the meal, he did not see her speak. She poured Sir Clive's tea only to be loudly berated for doing so, before the food arrived. "It'll be cold, dammit woman!"

Stewart couldn't stop thinking about Lady Harvey. Not because she was beautiful; she was, but because it seemed to him she was married to a bully and it brought back to him all the feelings of helplessness and frustration that he had felt when he had to face his own bullies. He had, in his mother's words, challenging looks, and had been tortured all his life by people who used his misfortune to appear witty and clever to others, making them laugh at his expense.

*

A couple of days later, Stewart asked if he could take his lunch out into the garden, to enjoy a little peace and quiet in the spring sunshine. The Manager agreed, but Stewart was to "retire inside" immediately if any guests appeared. Stewart guessed they were all out as the hotel was very quiet, so off he went armed only with sandwiches, his notebook and the treasured silver pencil which had belonged to his Father. Stewart quickly immersed himself in his writing, the little silver pencil darting this way and that and quickly filling the pages. He forgot all about his sandwiches, so engrossed was he, and so did not hear the delicate footsteps of Lady Harvey; he did not hear her settle herself at a nearby table in the sunshine, loosening her Hermes scarf as it was so warm. Nor did he see her open her book and start to read, her Dior glasses perched daintily on the end of her perfect nose. When Stewart came up for air from his scribblings and saw her, he gasped. How long had she been there? Oh, he would be for it now, he could only hope The Manager had not seen him. He quickly scrambled his belongings together and stood up to leave. Lady Harvey, however, was fully aware that he was there. She liked this odd, quiet young man, and, realising his isolation, was keen to get to know him better. She couldn't believe her luck at finding him in the garden where she had come to escape.

"Hello, Stewart," she greeted him warmly. "Have I disturbed you? I am so sorry!" She glanced at his untouched lunch, smiled her perfect smile and Stewart wondered how anyone could be unkind to such a lovely thing.

"No, not at all, I was just finished, I..." Stewart faltered, knowing he was not supposed to interact with the guests and, Lord above, he would get the sack, for certain, if The Manager saw this. He flushed bright red, and dropped his sandwich box and his pencil. As he bent forward to pick them up his glasses slipped down. He glanced up to see Lady Harvey leap out of her seat to help him, but she was a blur. He pushed his bulky glasses back up his long, thin nose so quickly the heavy frames dug into his flesh, cutting him and, as if he had not suffered indignity enough, he felt the blood slowly trickle down the side of his face. Stewart wanted the ground to open up and swallow him whole, wanted a bolt of lightning to end his misery as he fumbled now for his regulation issue white handkerchief, which seemed to have gone absent without leave. Before he could do anything about it, Lady Harvey was dabbing away gently at the crimson rivulet with her own handkerchief, its delightful, subtle fragrance making Stewart feel light-headed. Or was it the cut?

"Thank you," muttered Stewart through his embarrassment, "thank you. I really must go now, I am due back on duty and not allowed out here, and you are very kind, thank you." And with that he rushed off inside.

"Wait!" called an amused Lady Harvey, but it was too late, he was gone and she was left with his notebook in her hand. She flicked idly through it, looking for Stewart's last name so she could leave it for him at the desk. She couldn't just put 'Stewart' on the envelope, weren't they all called Stewart up here? She thought she overheard the cheeky one who was in love with himself saying he was a Stuart. Then something caught her eye, something in the notebook written in Stewart's neat hand, about a woman having the complexion of a rose petal. She read on, at first feeling guilty but soon becoming so absorbed in his beautiful stories and poems that she forgot all sense of time and propriety. As the sun weakened and a breath of cool air wafted over her she finally put down the notebook and sat back in her chair. Well. Some people were full of surprises. This young man certainly had hidden depths!

*

Stewart had deliberately asked for duties which

would not bring him into contact with Sir Clive and Lady Harvey for the following couple of days. He knew they were only staying until Thursday, and he thought he would manage to avoid them until then, such was his shame and embarrassment. He looked in the mirror at the wound on the side of his nose. If he took off his glasses, no matter how hard he peered in to the mirror, the cut was nowhere to be seen, but as soon as he replaced the thick, heavy lenses he was revealed once more in all his detestable glory. He loved his job where he was required to be invisible yet useful, an omnipresent ghost fulfilling the requirements of people more beautiful, more clever, more worthy than he. Stewart was not wallowing in self-pity, he was realistic about his prospects and his abilities, and his appearance, because like it or not, what you have to show to the world is how you are judged by others. Stewart felt that his world had collapsed when his cloak of invisibility had been lifted, showing all his fumbling failings and his ugliness coming under the close scrutiny of Lady Harvey. Worst of all, he could not find his notebook. He had been back to the garden but there was no sign of it there, he thought he might have dropped it in the staff area, but no luck. He was frantic in case one of the other members of staff found it. They would read it and he would be ridiculed all the more, passing it round and laughing like a pack of hyenas.

Worse was to come. Stewart returned to his

regular duties on Friday, determined to put his experience behind him and carry on as normal. As expected, Sir Clive and Lady Harvey were nowhere to be seen, so Stewart set about his duties with vigour. He served breakfast to a young, bohemian couple who, if he knew anything at all, looked as if they were still high, and who couldn't keep their hands off each other. They refused the table he offered them, instead asking him to prepare a recently vacated one in the window. Stewart drew his cloak of invisibility about him a little closer and obliged. The self-absorbed were blind, anyway. At lunchtime, The Manager approached Stewart.

"Here, Campbell, you are to take a couple of hours off this afternoon," he said curtly, looking none too pleased. Stewart realised he had been discovered, his accidental meeting with Lady Harvey had been seen after all. He flushed redder than he had ever done before, expecting at any moment to lose his job. He couldn't speak, he was so mortified. "You are wanted in the garden NOW!" The Manager continued, and turned sharply, disappearing into the kitchen and leaving Stewart mentally preparing for an encounter with the hotel owner. He made his way out into the spring sunshine, which blinded him temporarily so he couldn't see his accuser. Shading his eyes from the still low sun, he could see a figure seated at a table with its back to him. Oh well, here goes, he thought and strode across the garden. He approached the table, then stopped suddenly. It was Lady Harvey! He made a mental note to get on top of this blushing thing and said, "Oh, good afternoon Lady Harvey, I must apologise, I have mistaken you for someone else. I am so sorry," and Stewart was about to retreat when she said, "Yes, Stewart, that someone is me. Please sit down, I have something which I think belongs to you."

Stewart's heart was pounding in his chest. He must have upset her, he would definitely get the sack now. He was mentally trying to remember where the job centre was when he saw his notebook on the table. His failing, miserable eyes nearly popped out of his head. Again, the blushing.

"You left it behind in your haste to escape from me," Lady Harvey could see he was speechless, "and as you seem to have been absent from the hotel, I could not return it to you." She handed the notebook to Stewart.

"I thought you had left the hotel!" was Stewart's reply, and he was immediately struck by his appalling lack of manners. "Thank you, I'm so rude! Thank you so much. I thought I had lost it!" Stewart turned his precious book over and over in his hands.

"Well," Lady Harvey was struggling to hide her amusement, "we might have done if my husband had secured the funding for his latest project! He hasn't, so we are staying a while longer."

"Oh, I see," Stewart felt a little pleased at this. "I hope he is successful."

"So do I," replied Lady Harvey, with a

somewhat wry smile. "He's spent all my money on his ridiculous schemes. This is his last chance. Enough about him. I would like to talk to you about the contents of this little book. Oh, and how is your nose, you poor thing? I have done that so many times myself, see here, look at the scar," and she lifted her rose petal face to the sunlight so he could see. "I would like to say my contact lenses are the answer but they are not. I need these things too, my sight is so bad!" Stewart found himself laughing with her, comparing lack of sight and then they talked about his beloved Edinburgh, compared school experiences and finally discussed the contents of the little book.

"Where did you learn to write like this?" she wanted to know, and he could only tell her it came from inside, from his heart, from his head, he didn't really know where. All he knew was that he had desperately wanted to be a writer from childhood. Books had been his saviours, authors were the gods of the hallowed library temple and he was only really himself when he was scribbling. "I have loads of these books," he laughed easily with her, "sadly all numbered sequentially. I really need to get out more!" Stewart had never felt so normal, so alive and so utterly engaged in conversation and they chatted and laughed together for far longer than two hours. He could sense Lady Harvey's amusement, but he could also sense her delight in him for who he was rather than how he appeared. For the first time he had realised the beauty from within is the beauty which others see. Not everyone, but the ones who really matter.

"Let's have some tea, Stewart, then we can talk about what to do with all this lovely writing of yours!" Malcolm served them afternoon tea, bowing slightly as he retreated from the table and asking, "Is everything alright, Madam? And you, Sir?" He turned to Stewart and gave him a knowing wink, accompanied by the most mischievous smile Stewart had ever seen.

"Now," Lady Harvey said, "I know someone in London who will be able to point you in the right direction of a publisher. Do you think you could bring your work down?" She sipped her tea. Stewart was flushed with excitement. He really must get on top of this blushing thing. He looked up to see The Manager leaving the window, and it occurred to him that perhaps his whole life was not going to be here, hiding behind a cloak of invisibility, after all.

Alice's Garden

Josephine Esterling

Shielding her eyes from the early morning spring sun, Alice stood at the cottage gate and surveyed the land that she had bought. She wondered if her family were right: would it be too much for her? When she had told her friends and work colleagues that she was retiring to Yorkshire, they had been surprised, but wished her luck. Her family had been quite against it and even more so when she had told them she was going to make a garden. 'Mum, what do you know about gardening?' her eldest daughter had asked.

'Quite a bit, thank you,' Alice had replied, drawing her short slender figure up to its full height. 'If you remember the bit of garden we had when you were children, I grew lots of flowers and veg, and you kids had a go at growing Sun Flowers.'

'Yes, but that wasn't on the scale you are talking about. Three acres is a lot of ground. You're too old to do it,' her son had insisted. Feeling wounded by their lack of faith in her, Alice had tossed her cream-tinted curls and looked each of her three adult children in the eye over the top of her glasses. 'I have wanted a proper garden with clipped hedges, a pond and a veg plot since I was a

111

little girl helping my grandfather in his garden. Besides, I have hired a garden company to do the hard work for me.' Alice had dug her heels in, certain that she could do it. She had learnt a lot over the years from television programs and books. Eventually she had drawn her own designs. Now, after years of saving every penny possible and selling her flat, she had more than enough for the cottage and the garden. The neglected land would be hard going for the workmen, but Alice could imagine a path lined with trees winding its way from the simple, two-bedroomed cottage down to the river. In spring there would be daffodils and blue bells dancing in the wind between flowering shrubs. Later, anemone and creeping geranium and other perennials and annuals would carpet the ground. At the river, weeping willows would offer shade from the summer heat. There would be a seat set at the water's edge so she could watch the dragonflies in the reeds and flag irises. She imagined the great-grandchildren dipping their nets into the rushing water, their happy voices echoing around the garden. Even in winter their laughter would send snow cascading from laden trees, and when they were gone, the sound would still linger in the glass house and around the maze.

Alice stamped her foot. 'Come what may, I shall have a garden.' She fiddled with the rusty gate catch, her arthritic fingers not as nimble as they once were, and stepped out onto the dew-soaked scrub. She had an image of a fine-cut lawn laid out before her with the path bordering it. In the middle would be a large magnolia with pink flower buds standing like candles in its branches. At Christmas she could put tea light candles in coloured glass holders in its branches. Alice giggled. It would be like a real candle tree.

She took, from a basket over her arm, little wooden stakes and marked out the lawn. She joined the stakes up with a can of white spray paint. Then she added a marker for the magnolia and wrote her idea in a notebook, so that later she could draw it on the plans for the garden. She measured and marked out the path to the river, then added other paths. One to the rose garden with its tea lawn and summer house smothered in sweet smelling honeysuckle and a white rambling rose. It would be a peaceful place to retreat to when the weather was wet. A wood stove, she wrote in the notebook, for when it was chilly. Another path would lead to the herb garden and walled fruit and vegetable garden near the cottage, so that she could just pop out and pick what she needed. This path would pass by long, deep, mixed boarders edged with dwarf lavender.

Alice marked out a children's area where a large, old, stumpy oak stood. Its branches would be perfect for climbing. The plants here, like deep purple buddleia, would attract insects. She made a note to put a bird table here as well, and a table with bench seats that the children would like.

Alice worked all day. She marked out a maze of box hedging and topiary with a fountain in the middle. She stopped only for a quick cup of tea and a sandwich which she made in the cottage kitchen. She had barely unpacked her belongings from moving in the day before. She had taken out only those things she needed from the many boxes stashed amongst her furniture around the cottage. The garden was more important than anything else, especially as it was early spring and things would be starting to grow.

In the late afternoon, Alice sat by the river and put the final notes on her plans for the garden. 'Perfect', she whispered to a passing kingfisher hunting for his tea, 'just perfect.'

The contractors came across Alice the next morning. She had sent them a basic set of plans for the garden weeks before and, because they could see the garden had been clearly marked out, they had started the work on the hard landscaping. Her body was found lying on a picnic blanket, the notebook on her lap. The plans were spread out beside her, held down with stones, a dreamy smile on her face.

The Desk

Paula Harrison

I like my walking. I usually walk with a group but this particular day I just wanted my own company. No particular reason. It was a fine summer day so I packed a picnic and a map in my rucksack and set off.

It was not totally familiar ground but I headed for the high moors. I enjoyed the peace, solitude and isolation. The heather was blooming, the scent filling the air on the warm southerly breeze. Bees buzzed from the nearby hives. I came across a track marked on the map so I continued. The only company that I had were the sheep and a lonely buzzard gliding across a cloudless sky.

I came to a dwelling, the existence of which was vaguely familiar to me. I checked the map: it was marked, but had no name. There was no sign of life. The garden was overgrown with brambles and thistles, the remains of a board with the words 'High Fell Farm' just discernible lying in the undergrowth. Many years ago this must have been a much-loved cottage garden, a blaze of colour with the foxgloves, poppies, lupins and hollyhocks that now struggled to survive in this jungle. I ventured through a rotting wooden gate held together by a rusty hinge, the sneck having corroded away years ago. I stood for a moment. Beneath the nettles and brambles was a garden path leading to a lean-to shed full of decomposing logs; its corrugated metal roof was rusty and full of holes. On the house itself, broken guttering and fall pipes hung precariously from a roof devoid of most of its tiles. How the recent winters must have taken their toll on this lonely dwelling. The chimney stack had partially collapsed, and a crow had made its home in the only remaining chimney pot. House martins nested peacefully under the eaves, darting in and out of their nests to catch unwary insects for their young.

Curious, I looked through a broken window. A pigeon had nested in an old cupboard. The hinges had rusted away and the door lay on the floor. The old Yorkist range looked remarkably intact. Gales and storms had sent soot down the chimney; it covered most of what was left of the floor. I wondered who had cooked on this range. Who were they? Where did they get their food? I stumbled to the back of the house through the nettles, thistles, dog mercury; the weeds were taller than me. I was glad of my walking boots and stick. I wiped the moss off a kitchen window and I saw the damp red and black quarry tiles covering an uneven floor which was in turn covered with plaster that had fallen from the walls. A Belfast sink stood heavily on crumbling brick supports, a cold water tap loosely attached to corroding pipes.

I looked back over the garden to an orchard

with apple, pear and cherry trees. There was a former vegetable garden with rows of frames that had seen better days, gooseberry bushes and raspberry canes, once neatly tended and cared for but now forgotten. Nature had taken its course. I fought my way through the orchard to a stable. The doors and roof had collapsed decades ago. A heavy horse collar hung from a hook, the straw hanging from the leather. Rusting farm implements from a former age were scattered on the cracked concrete floor.

I looked at my watch: 11:05. Plenty of time for this easy walk, so I ventured into the house. I pushed the door which opened easily into a porchway. An old mildewed, holey, gaberdine mac hung on a rusty hook, a walking stick and old boots placed neatly underneath. I was really curious now. I wondered if anyone might still live here.

Silence.

I crept through the hall way into a sitting room. I knew that I shouldn't be there. I was a trespasser. I felt guilty. The door was heavy. It took all my strength to push it open. It creaked, but opened enough for me to squeeze through. There was no sunlight on this side of the farm. It took me a moment to readjust to the light, so I just stood.

In the silence and shadow of the sitting room was a figure. I was shocked to the core of my existence. It was a soldier. I couldn't move, speak or ask questions. The colour must have drained from my face. I was terrified, rooted to the spot. I wanted to run away, but the door was only just wide enough for me to squeeze through. I looked again. The soldier had two stripes on his uniform, "a corporal," I thought, "and the uniform is not a modern one, but clearly it is British." The corporal spoke.

"Good morning, we don't have many visitors," he said. I stood, transfixed by what I was seeing and hearing. The house had seemed to be derelict and empty, and yet I was being addressed by someone who was apparently living there.

He stood up. "I am just ending my leave. I am going back to the front line on the Somme later today."

The Somme? My mind was working overtime now. I recognised the uniform, it was from The Great War.

"Let me show you round. Let's start in the kitchen."

The kitchen was no longer derelict. A pheasant hung from a hook on a beam, a well scrubbed table and four chairs stood on a clippy mat. A welsh dresser had cooking pots, crockery, meat plates of a bygone era. Eggs, flour, butter, meat adorned the table ready for a good baking day. Everything was clean, white, washed and cared for. An elderly lady in a white apron was busying herself with the general chores you'd find in any kitchen. "My mother keeps this kitchen impeccable," he said, winking at her. "She loves baking for the family."

But my mind floundered for explanations. Was this time travel? Had I gone back in time? Had he come forward? The idea was crazy, but the evidence was all around me. Or maybe this was all a dream, or a hallucination.

We passed through a little hallway into an office. An oil lamp stood in a recess next to the fire. Several candles stood in polished brass candlesticks on the desk. "I like drawing," said my host. "I keep my drawings in this desk. I have a sense of peace at home. Here, look at these. This is the farm in winter, and in the summer, the garden, the stable, the orchard. This is my dad with the sheep and Trixie, the border collie; and May, the Shire horse out in the fields with Dad." The detail and colour were impeccable.

"Let's continue." I followed him in a daze of confusion. We left the house through a side door into the orchard. Neat rows of logs stood next to the house. In the orchard, the grass had been cut into hay and was stacked ready for winter. The horse looked over the stable door, and we went inside. Well-oiled tack and ploughing gear hung on the walls; kittens played in the hay bales catching imaginary mice. We walked through the vegetable garden where there was enough produce for the entire winter.

The sun, almost due south at this time of day, cast bright rays across the garden. I turned. There was no one there. I was alone. I looked again at my surroundings, transfixed. The farm was just as it had been when I'd arrived, with holes in the roof, and the overgrown garden; the house was derelict, silent and forgotten. I couldn't understand what had happened. I had no explanation. I stood there, but time didn't seem to have any meaning. A gentle breeze whispered through the trees. I was brought back to the present by the sudden movement of a sparrowhawk swooping through the garden before soaring up over the distant moorland.

I left the farm. It was not long before I was sitting on a rock having my lunch. I was surrounded by open moorland and looking down on the farm from a different angle. I reflected upon the morning's events. Were they real? Was it the light casting shadows? Had I invented it all? Had I been asleep and dreamt everything? I thought about spirits, but I didn't really know what the term meant. I was unable to explain it or come to a logical conclusion and began to have doubts about the whole event.

I continued my walk, my thoughts returning to the corporal and his drawings, but failing to understand why, or even *if* it had happened.

Then there was a feeling to return to the old farm – not so much a feeling but more of a compulsion. I had to go back. As I walked over the hill the farm came into view. I quickened my pace, curious yet wary. What had happened this morning? The farm was empty, derelict, silent. There was no sign of life. I ventured inside – no farmer's wife cooking, no army corporal. The place was neglected, empty, forgotten. I crept into the study. The old desk stood there, dusty and faded. I opened a drawer. Inside was a discoloured telegram. I unfolded it and read the brief massage: 'Corporal William Baines missing believed dead'. There was also an obituary in a yellowing newspaper cutting which read, 'William Baines aged 27, lived at High Fell Farm, killed in action, Arras, 15th September 1916'. That was 99 years ago today.

I thought to myself, I can't tell anyone about this, they will think that I am insane. The corporal was real though. I opened the drawer. His paintings were intact. They were dirty and faded, but complete. I had intruded enough. I returned the paintings, closed the drawer and left full of thoughts and unanswered questions.

*

The weeks passed. I had to go back. I walked quickly through the heather to High Fell Farm. There was a van outside and a family looking at the farm. I hesitated and passed the time of day. I was going to leave but I wanted to know more so I engaged in conversation. I explained that I lived locally and occasionally passed the farm. The chap, who seemed vaguely familiar, wasn't English. He told me that he was from Northern France and that his name was Emile. He was pleasant and introduced me to his wife, Angela, who was an artist, and their two children. He explained that he had been doing some family research and found that his great-great-grandmother had had a child out of wedlock to a British soldier. I instinctively knew that the father was Corporal William Baines; seeing Emile's face, mannerisms and voice was like looking back through time.

He went on to say that as part of his research he had come across a press cutting that mentioned High Fell Farm and that he had decided to visit. "It's a forgotten place now," he said sadly.

Emile took out a folder and showed me the press cutting: 'William Baines aged 27, lived at High Fell Farm, killed in action, Arras, 15th September 1916'. The photograph left me in no doubt as to who had shown me round the farm earlier that year. I looked at the photo and looked at Emile, the likeness was uncanny.

Angela asked me to accompany them. "Let's go inside." I felt that I was intruding but they insisted. I also felt that I was being trusted with a secret from my mysterious day.

I explained that I had been curious one day and ventured inside. The family seemed not to mind, and were instead rather interested. As they approached the desk and the secrets that it held, it was mysteriously locked. Emile and his wife were indifferent to this but I was mystified. I began to say that I had looked in the drawer on my previous visit but I bit my lip and said nothing.

We continued the tour, the family explaining they were leaving France. Emile was a builder and wanted now to return to High Fell Farm and after much wrangling, time wasting and red tape, he was now the owner. They explained their plans to me, a perfect stranger. They wanted to keep the original features and 'bring back the past.' Angela had plans for the orchard and garden.

I was fascinated by their plans and was happy when they asked me to call again, pleased to have a local link.

*

It was late autumn when I next passed the farm. Building work was evident: the building was surrounded by scaffolding, the roof was covered in plastic sheeting and there were stones and planks of wood all over the orchard. Emile saw me and welcomed me.

"I need a break," he smiled. He explained his work was progressing well. He wanted to keep the range and the quarry tiles. We walked into the study. "My job this morning is to chop this desk up and burn it. "

"No!" I exclaimed. Emile looked surprised. "Please don't."

"It won't fit through the door, which is probably why no one's ever taken it away. We can't open the drawers without causing a lot of damage, so it has to go."

"Please," I implored Emile, "please let us have another go at opening the drawer?"

Emile smiled. "Angela!" he shouted. Angela appeared at the door. "For some reason, Ann

doesn't want us to throw the old desk away."
Angela didn't respond but started to show her
plans to me.

"I've been sketching garden plans." I looked
twice, the detail, colour and images were just as I'd
been shown by Corporal William Baines. I was still
wondering why the drawer was locked. I asked
again if I could try to open it.

"Okay," said Emile dismissively, "give it another
go." I tried the drawer, and to everyone's surprise,
including my own, it moved slightly. We
persevered and eventually it opened. The drawer
contained papers that smelt a bit musty. We lifted
them out and to my amazement the dusty, faded
sketches and drawings that I had seen a few
months earlier were still intact. There was a
silence. We laid the drawings out on the desk.
Angela was intrigued by the detail of the garden
pictures. Emile was excited by the intricate images
of the interior of each room and studied them with
stunned disbelief.

When the silence was finally broken, Emile
said, smiling, "That was certainly worth the effort.
Thank you, Ann. We would have lost these forever
if the desk had gone." He turned to Angela. "I
think we might have our house plans completed
here."

"Well, it certainly looks as if these drawings
might have just about completed the garden
plans," said Angela.

"This study feels like a shrine to Corporal

William Baines. It's as if his family never came to terms with his death. He was an only son and, according to my family research, he was to inherit the farm." Emile went on to say that he felt peaceful here, like coming home. His research had not found any evidence of anyone living here after the parents had died. I agreed, saying that I had only ever known it as a ruin. I was about to leave as the daylight was fading.

"What about the old desk?" I asked.

"You and that desk," Emile laughed. "Well, we can't get it out so I suppose it will have to stay."

On my way home I thought about the day's events. I couldn't explain them. Was I mad? Was I a messenger? Had I invented the whole story?

*

I was busy over the next few months so it was quite some time before I was back at High Fell Farm. The transformation was breathtaking. I thought of Corporal William Baines's paintings of the farm in the summer. I felt that I had gone back in time nearly a hundred years. Emile and Angela saw me, gave me a shout and invited me in. The range in the kitchen was burning brightly. Angela had just baked six loaves of bread. The welsh dresser was full of jams, pickles and chutneys. Angela confided that she liked using old recipes. There was the table and four chairs on a clippy mat. In the front room a fire burned logs, occasionally spitting red sparks into the hearth. On the wall hung the drawings. Angela explained that she had recreated them from the dusty, faded ones in the desk. The originals were stored away safely to minimise damage.

"Right, you," Emile joked. "Close your eyes. In here." He led me into the next room. "Right, open them now." I looked round and saw a new desk where the old one had been.

"Why did you throw the desk out?" I asked disappointedly.

"I didn't. That's it. Restored, polished, new brass hinges all to the original detail. Look." Emile held up the press cutting and telegram in an appropriate frame. "I found this wedged at the back." He held up a regal-looking case containing war medals. I felt as if I was being shown around again by Corporal William Baines.

"Hurry up, Emile," said Angela. "I want to show her the garden."

"Angela," I asked, "there was an old coat, boots and crook by that door."

"As an artist," she replied, "it caught my attention. I did this etching of them here. The coat's in the stable."

Angela and Emile took me round the garden. There were neat rows of vegetables, fruit bushes and flowers, exactly as Corporal William Baines had shown me. The stable had been rebuilt, the old farm implements polished and hung on the wall, the horse collar restored by Angela.

"We both feel like we have come home. Sometimes I feel a peaceful presence," said Emile, "as if we are supposed to be here." I had my back to the stable looking down the garden. In the evening light three figures smiled, waved and faded into the shadows: a farmer in a gaberdine mac, his wife in an apron and Corporal William Baines in full military uniform.

"Yes." I said with feeling. "You've come home."

Together Again

Caroline Stewart

Clare hadn't lived in the area long but felt very much at home there. It was nice to have a clean break, to start again and to keep all those skeletons firmly locked up in the closet. No-one here knew her past and no-one judged her because of it. She walked along the cinder path to the village where she picked up a few essentials for the weekend. She wouldn't be going far, so just some milk, a frozen pizza for tea and a bottle of wine. She stopped, as usual, to read the cards in the window of the Co-op. She was always on the lookout for old lawn mowers or gadgets she could repair. It was her favourite pastime and she knew the villagers had nicknamed her Mrs Fixer. She didn't mind at all.

There was nothing doing today so she headed home as the sun began to set. By the time she reached the back door fifteen minutes later it was dark. She fished in her pocket for her keys and cursed the awful sodium lamp the council had helpfully installed outside the back of her house. It was so low that it cast her shadow onto the door making it impossible to see what she was doing. She managed to fumble the key into the lock and went in, locking the door behind her. She was in for the night. Most women her age would have been getting ready to go out on the town at that time on a Saturday night, but she was happy to be staying in to work on her latest restoration project: a 1940's black Bakelite GPO telephone.

She'd had the thing working and had tested it earlier in the day, but being the perfectionist she was, there were a couple of things that weren't up to scratch. The dial needed to come out for a service as it wasn't quite right, but first she wanted to replace the old braided cable. She turned on some music, settled down with a drink and began tinkering with the old phone.

A couple of hours later she awoke with a start. She must have fallen asleep sitting next to the fire. She blinked, confused. What was that noise? She looked down at the black telephone next to her. It was ringing. A shrill, piercing sound that rattled around her half-asleep head. She instinctively reached down and picked up the heavy old receiver. "Hello," she mumbled, trying to sound more alert than she felt.

"Hi, it's me," a distant voice said. "Are you coming down to ours tonight? We're all here. We were expecting you. We're in the bottom field with a nice bonfire going."

Her mind began racing. Who was it? What bonfire? The voice was vaguely familiar but, embarrassed at not being able to recognise who it was, she bluffed her way out. "Sorry, I must have nodded off. I'm on my way. See you in a few minutes," and she replaced the handset into the cradle.

She jumped up and threw on a coat. She was about to dash out when she remembered the fire. She never left the fire unguarded, even when she was at home, but she always had to double check the old fashioned guard was in place before she left the room. Tonight she propped an old railway lamp in front of it to ensure it couldn't move if anything rolled out of the fire.

Her head still swimming she glanced once more round the room. The fire was safe and she would clear up the telephone and all her tools later. As she turned and left the room she squinted at the telephone feeling sure that she hadn't finished it. If she had looked more closely she would have noticed that the old phone she'd just answered wasn't connected to anything. That job was still to do and where it should have been plugged into the telephone socket there was tangle of coloured wires, twisted together like the branches of a tree.

She opened the back door and was greeted by the awful sodium-bathed night. The street light seemed to be brighter than ever and the air was misted with a sulphurous smoke from the bonfire. It rasped her throat as she gulped in the cold evening air. She fumbled her way into the street, rubbing her face with her hands, trying to wake herself up. She knew it was a full moon tonight and threw back her head to try to see it. She could see neither the moon nor the stars because that too bright street lamp overpowered her eyes. She hated that light and had often vowed to shoot it out with an air rifle. She glared angrily at it before turning to head down the street. The second she did so the light went out with a loud pop, plunging her into darkness.

"At last," she said wryly to herself and paused to allow her eyes to get used to the darkness. That was when she heard the voices, laughing and talking. She spotted the glow in the bottom field and saw the sparks jumping into the night sky. She could now smell the woodsmoke, and heard her name being called above the crackling of the fire.

Without giving her eyes a proper chance to become accustomed to the dark, she headed down the street, stumbling over the sleeping policeman at the bottom of the road. It was as if she was being drawn towards the voices. Her mind was trying to resist. *Go back inside, it's late*, a concerned voice inside her head told her, but her legs had other ideas. Increasingly uncomfortable, she got closer to the bottom field where she could make out the silhouettes of three people around the bonfire.

She heard her name being called again by that voice, "Hurry up Clare, we're waiting for you."

At that moment the name, the face came into her head. It was as if someone had gripped her heart with an icy hand. She felt every trace of happiness disappear from her being to be replaced by a terrifying fear. Again, she heard her name and, although every muscle in her body wanted to turn and run, she couldn't. She was drawn like a magnet towards these people and the fire. The gate opened and her legs carried her through the field towards the fire where the silhouette of three figures was picked out by the angry flickering flames. None of the girls in the group acknowledged her or even turned to look at her, but even from behind she knew who they were. They were still wearing the clothes they'd worn the last time she saw them, on that fateful night out in town.

The light of the fire caught a necklace one of them was wearing and she recognised it as her own. She remembered that as they'd all got ready to go out that night as they did together very Friday night, she had lent it to her friend Bev, who in return had lent her a pair of tight, black satin trousers. They had all gone out together, had a few, well a lot of drinks, danced and had a wonderful night. They had a rule when they went out that they never ever split up. Even if one of them hooked up with a bloke, they always went home together. It had kept them safe over the years even though it caused a few arguments when three of them dragged the fourth out of the arms of her new flame. But on that particular night it had all gone wrong. The events that she had tried so hard to forget came flooding back to her as if it was yesterday. She recalled that when it was time to go, having had a bit too much to drink, she had wanted to get some chips to take home. The other three had reluctantly agreed to wait in the rowdy queue while she bought her chips then went to the taxi that they had booked beforehand. The driver was annoyed that he'd been sitting waiting and the others, obviously a bit peeved, said very little but got in. She was last to climb into the car. As she closed the door the driver spotted the chips and pointed to the sign forbidding food. He was in no mood for negotiation and to avoid a row she jumped out of the taxi calling after the others that she'd finish her food and get a taxi home on her own. The other three insisted "We all go home together." As the car pulled away, Clare could still hear the protests of the other girls, but the driver was having none of it, already late for his next pick up he wasn't about to start bending the rules for her.

She walked along the street a little worse for wear but knowing that the large portion of chips she had would help to reduce the effects of the inevitable hangover in the morning. Although the intensity of the headache might be lessened she knew the ear-bashing she would receive from the girls for breaking their pact would be at full volume. It wasn't a long walk, but they always got a taxi because their carefully constructed Friday night outfits of high heels and no coats weren't ideal for a fifteen minute walk and the route home did pass through a few lonely areas that weren't particularly nice to walk through alone. But, buoyed by the over-confidence provided by too much drinking, she wandered towards home, eating her chips.

She had left the bustle of the late night revellers and was walking through a dimly lit street, still devouring her late night snack. It was only when she finished her food and started to look around for a bin that she saw him. The man who had been waiting on the corner in the shadow of the telephone box and had slipped into step behind her a few minutes earlier. As she turned and looked he stopped and bent down, seemingly to tie his lace. A cold anxiety started to infiltrate her thoughts and, still clutching the empty chip wrapper, she carried on trying to walk a little faster.

The route home was about to take Clare through an even darker side street and, feeling increasingly uneasy, she casually turned back to see if the man was still behind me. To her horror, he was even closer and had pulled up his hood. There was no alternative to the dark alley but it was quite short and led into the street next to where she lived. Looking round she saw the man doing the same, checking there was no-one about. Clare decided to make a run for it and, dropping her chip papers, she ran as hard as she could down the alley. She didn't need to turn, she could hear the pounding of his feet on the cobbles behind her. She stumbled, but kept her feet despite her heels, and made it through the alley into the street of friendly houses. But she was far from safe. She kept running, aware that he was gaining on her. As she rounded the corner into her own street, she almost flattened a man walking his dog. She practically cried with joy as she realised it was her neighbour, Billy, talking his little terrier for a walk before turning in.

"Steady on, Clare!" he exclaimed. "What's the hurry?"

Barely able to breathe, she forced a smile, put her hand on Billy's arm for support and turned around. The man had gone. Disappeared back into the darkness. She blew out a long sigh. "I just had a bit of a fright, Billy, but I'm ok now. Can I walk back with you?"

When she got in, her parents were still awake. She made some story up about getting a taxi back by herself and crawled into bed. Clare decided not to mention this to the girls. She would never hear the last of it and they would make her report it to the police and then she'd be in trouble with her parents for getting drunk and walking home alone, especially after she'd just lied about getting a taxi. No, Clare would keep this to herself, but she would never again leave the safety of her friends after a night out.

She awoke in the morning feeling sick with a hangover. She briefly felt a pang of fear as she recalled the frightening walk home and again vowed never to walk home on her own. She went downstairs to be met by the solemn faces of her parents. At first she thought that Billy had told them how scared she'd been and she was going to get a telling off for walking home alone. But it was much, much worse than that. Her mother started to cry as her father sat her down and handed her a cup of strong, sweet tea.

"What? What is it?" she asked, a knot beginning to form in her stomach.

"There was an accident last night, Clare," he whispered as if saying it quietly would lessen the impact. She felt the nausea rising and clasped her hand over her mouth, eyes widening. "It's bad news, Clare, very bad news," he continued gravely. Her eyes slowly moved from her father's to her mother's face. Her mother clutched a sodden piece of kitchen towel to her eyes and shook her head.

"Just tell me," Clare hissed. Her father took a deep breath and in a matter of fact voice began. "Clare, the taxi that the girls came home in last night was involved in a nasty accident. You know that bad corner at the far end of town, before the supermarket?" She nodded wide-eyed. He continued, his voice now wavering. "Apparently there were witnesses who said the taxi was going far too fast. It missed the bend and the car turned over and caught fire."

"Oh no, how are they? The girls? How are the girls?" she whimpered.

Her father looked down and took a deep breath. "It was an inferno, Clare. No-one had a chance."

She couldn't really remember the next few days. She lay in her room going over that night again and again. It was her fault. If she hadn't had too much to drink and needed some food, the driver wouldn't have been angry at being late and driven too fast, trying to make his next pick up in time. Not only did she have the death of the driver on her conscience, but worse still the deaths of her three best friends. She should've died too.

Clare had to go to the inquest and say what had happened in the run-up to the accident. When the papers printed the story, they as much as said the driver had been speeding to make up time because Clare had held them up by going to the takeaway. She thought that too. Everyone thought that. She could tell. People stared at her, shunned her. She felt like an outcast. Everywhere she went there was something to remind her of the girls or the accident. If only she could go back in time and fix everything.

It was making her ill, and eventually she was so unhappy she made the move away from the place she grew up. She moved to the village where she began to invent a new life for herself. The accident had changed her. No longer was she confident around people. She struggled to make new friends as she couldn't talk about her past. She developed strange habits which she learned to live with but that others found strange. It had taken her years to learn to live with the guilt and she'd only managed this by burying it and all her memories far away in the back of her mind.

Now here she was, in a field with the three dead girls, still wearing their Friday night clothes. They turned to look at her and she recoiled in horror. Although their clothes were just as they were the last time she'd seen them, their faces were barely recognisable. Burnt and charred. Their arms were black and in places the flesh was completely burnt away exposing bones, browned with the heat of the car fire. Bev, wearing that necklace round her blackened neck spoke: "Hello Clare. You shouldn't stare. We know we look terrible, don't we?" They nodded, and then, in unison, said calmly, "We had a rule - we stick together. You broke that rule."

She tried to speak, to explain, to tell them what had happened and to apologise but nothing came out of her mouth. She wanted them to know that they were right. They should've stuck together and she had tortured herself with regrets since that terrible night.

"We stick together," they chanted as they lined up behind her. She turned, the heat from the fire now on her back. "We stick together," over and over again. Their gruesome faces smiled at her as they approached her. She stepped backwards away from them. "Together again," they grinned, their white teeth contrasting with their blackened complexions. Gnarled hands like burnt sticks reached out to her and again she stepped back knowing that she was edging ever closer to the bonfire. She felt the heat on her back. Warm at first but then hot, too hot. "Together again, together again, together again," and her legs carried her into the flames, searing pain as her feet sank into the embers. Her mouth opened wide, trying to scream, but no sound came out. The roar of the flames almost drowned out the voices, still chanting as the smell of burning flesh mixed with the woodsmoke. Her eyes began to lose focus but she could see the charred faces who watched her burn, just as they had themselves.

Project Juliette

Antony Wootten

Hugo awoke from some very strange dreams. His head was still full of unfamiliar voices saying uncatchable things when the alarm went off. He reached over and silenced it. He turned to his wife, Juliette, who was lying on her side, her back to him. He put his arm across her slender body and she groaned, as reluctant as him to emerge into the world.

A few minutes later, Hugo was showered and dressed, and sitting in the kitchen of their spacious apartment. Outside, an orange sun was trying to burn through the city's smog. Nearby trees and buildings were just grey blurs. He sipped coffee, absent-mindedly positioning his buttery knife so that its tip was in the dead centre of his plate. Juliette, still in her dressing gown, switched the radio on for some quiet background music.

"Anything special happening today, love?" Hugo said, and took a bite of toast.

"Not really," Juliette replied, her dark eyes glittering beneath the kitchen light. She was considerably younger than Hugo, and her loveliness awed him. She was in Artificial Intelligence software sales, and her job involved taking public transport across the city to different clients' places of work. "Got a few meetings, and a bit of a journey, but I shouldn't be back too late. Probably before you. Is it a normal day for you?"

"It's always a normal day for me," he said. "Right, better be off." He dropped an unwanted crust in the bin and placed his plate in the dishwasher. He nipped into the bathroom and gave his teeth their second clean of the day. He returned to the kitchen just as Juliette was giving instructions to the maid: "Please give the floors a mop while we're out," she was saying, "and if you could clean the balcony windows, that would be great. I don't know how the pigeons manage to poo on a vertical pane of glass, but they do." This last sentence was said to Hugo, not the maid. He and Juliette smiled, hugged, kissed.

"See you later, love," he said.

"Have a good day, babe," she replied.

"You too." Turning to the maid, Hugo said, "And you, Cynth. Enjoy scraping shit off windows." Cynthia, a boxy, white domestic droid with a cartoon face on a face-shaped screen, winked and said, "I sure will!"

As he left the flat, Hugo wondered about Cynthia. What went on behind that screen? It sometimes seemed quite human in what it said, but he knew it was all an act. Clever programming. But, he wondered as he made his way toward the lift, what kind of algorithm – what mathematical formula – was so complex that it could recognise humour? He pressed the button and waited for the lift to arrive. Even if droids were inert on the inside, it fascinated him to wonder how their minds worked. If he'd not gone into power-unit design, he'd have loved to have gone into Artificial Intelligence. He felt he'd have been quite good at it.

The lift doors hissed open and he stepped inside between two tall, young guys in blue boiler suits. He'd never seen either of them before, and their boiler suits instantly made him feel uneasy. This was a residential block. It was rare to see a boiler suits here. Anxiety rose in his throat as the doors closed, removing his opportunity to walk away. He forced a smile and a friendly greeting.

"Look at this," one of them said to him, and held up nothing but his index finger. Too late, Hugo realised this was a decoy. Behind him, the other man suddenly pressed something cold against the back of Hugo's neck, and the world disappeared.

*

"Hi, Cynthia," Hugo said when he returned home that evening.

"How was your day, Hugo?" the robot replied.

"Boring," Hugo said. It was. Just another day at the office. "Is Juliette in yet?"

"Hi, love," came Juliette's welcoming voice as she emerged from the bedroom, already in her pyjamas.

The evening was uneventful and relaxed, just the way they liked it. Cynthia cooked them a mild curry followed by a fruit crumble for dessert, and they chatted about their days, and their dreams for the future. They were planning on up-scaling from their apartment to a house, somewhere out of the city, where future pets and children could have all the space they needed.

It was late when they went to bed. The lights went out, and they fell asleep to the sound of Cynthia tinkering in the living-room.

*

Hugo awoke from some very strange dreams. His head was still full of unfamiliar faces wearing unreadable expressions when the alarm went off. He reached over and silenced it. Juliette stirred, already awake, and she stroked his face with her soft fingers.

Juliette was a university lecturer, and by her own admission, was woefully unprepared for this morning's nine-o'clock lecture on the history of democracy in the western world. She showered quickly, kissed Hugo goodbye, and hurried off without any breakfast, which was not unusual. Hugo, as always, did have time for breakfast. Absent-mindedly adjusting his unused spoon so that it was perfectly perpendicular to the table's edge, he chewed toast as the droid, Cynthia, served him coffee. Hugo wondered what the droid was thinking. How could it formulate thoughts? What algorithms enabled it to distinguish objects as entities separate from the surface they were on or the background it viewed them against? What

143

mathematics went on in its processors, enabling it to interpret human expressions and tones of voice?

No time to think about that today. He finished his breakfast, thanked the droid, wished it a pleasant day, and headed out. He stepped into the lift, his mind full of the dreams he could be living if he'd not got himself stuck in the rut of power-unit design, and found himself between two strangers in blue boiler suits. This unnerved him, but the lift doors closed before he could walk away.

"Mate," one of the men said, "have I got something in my teeth?" Too late, Hugo realised this was a decoy. Behind him, the other man suddenly pressed something cold against the back of Hugo's neck, and the world disappeared.

*

In the cramped observation room the air was thick with the smell of coffee and BO.

"Christ, it stinks in here," Quentin said as he entered. "Have you two been here all night?"

"He has," said Tory, a middle-aged woman with an overly-lined face and long hair that was incongruously ginger, except for its silvery roots. "I only came in a few minutes ago. Blame him for the smell."

"It's my hormones," said Blaine, a pretence at wide-eyed helplessness on his young, slender face. "What can I say?" This was noble of him; he and Hugo both knew Tory was the culprit.

"So, how's everything looking?" Quentin asked,

glancing at the screen as he helped himself to a cup of water from the cooler. "All good?" He sipped his water and watched the image in which Ten, a slender and attractive android which looked perfectly human, was striding along the street to a waiting taxi.

"All good. She's a university lecturer today."

"Yes, yes," Quentin said, "I know. It'll be a real test."

"It certainly will," said Tory. "I was really impressed with how she handled the sales role yesterday," she added. "She dealt with some difficult questions just like a real person. It was almost creepy!"

"Can we stop calling it 'her' please?" Quentin said, rubbing an antibacterial wipe over the chair he was about to sit in. "It's 'Ten'. Or 'it'," he asserted.

"Sure," Tory conceded. "But sometime she – *it* – has *me* fooled."

"Well, that's good," Quentin said, sitting gingerly and dropping the wipe in the bin.

"It's a testament to your work, Quentin," Blaine said, and then looked embarrassed, aware of how sycophantic that sounded.

Quentin quickly changed the subject. "Remind me, what have we got in store for poor old Hugo today?"

"Just another day at the office," Blaine announced, theatrically. "Some people have all the fun."

"Can't wait," said Quentin.

*

Half way through Hugo's day at the office, he went for lunch. He pushed open the door to the canteen, and found himself not in the canteen but in a huge, dark, empty space. Hugo stopped dead in his tracks. The canteen was simply not there, and neither was anything else.

He turned round, and headed for the door through which he'd come: it alone was still there, standing upright in the black space like a stage prop. But, as he approached it, it seemed to move away from him, always keeping just out of reach. He was in a panic now; what was happening? Had he lost his mind? He turned round and round, desperately searching for something familiar, but saw only darkness.

"Hugo," came a sudden voice. It came from the air all around him, and he found himself collapsing onto the hard, invisibly black floor. "Listen to me very carefully," the voice said. He recognised it, but couldn't pin it down. "What I'm about to tell you is incredibly important. You must do exactly as I say." Hugo opened his mouth but the voice continued. "At three AM tonight, the fire alarm in your block will go off. However, there will be no fire. But if you and Juliette do not leave the apartment, the consequences will be horrific. So, you must get out immediately. But do not use the lift or the stairs. Instead, go straight to apartment 304 and follow the escape route I've planned for you. Apartment 304."

"Who are you?" Hugo cried, his voice shaking. And suddenly he realised the disembodied voice sounded just like his own.

It continued: "I say again, apartment 304. Two doors along your corridor on the right. Do not go anywhere else."

"What's happening?" Hugo managed, getting to his feet again, but the voice allowed him no time to speak. It seemed to have been pre-recorded, but Hugo certainly had not made the recording himself.

"When the alarm goes at 3 AM, take Juliette and run. You will have no time to spare. Do not get dressed. Run to apartment 304 – it will open for you. On your arm will be a string of letters and numbers. It's not there now, and it won't be until you get home. Don't check. Don't let it be seen. But when you get to apartment 304, read it to Juliette. After that, things will get a bit strange, but you must trust Juliette and do what she says from that moment onwards. You will find a rucksack which I've left there for you. Take it but don't look in it until you are out of the building. Do what Juliette says. She will take you to my car. Once you are there, look in the rucksack. Time will be against you."

"Jesus, what?"

"In a minute," the recording continued, "you will find yourself back in the canteen. You must not show any sign of fear or alarm. You must act as if nothing has happened. You are being watched, everywhere. Go about the rest of your day as normal. Tonight, you must not say a word to anyone. Even in your flat, you are being watched. Say nothing to Juliette or to Cynthia."

Suddenly, the canteen reappeared and someone was barging past him in the doorway.

For the rest of the day, Hugo found himself in a whirl of confusion, an internal panic which it took him all his mental strength to conceal. Finally, he arrived home, but even then he couldn't relax. Juliette was not yet home, but Cynthia was there asking him about his day. He tried to behave as if nothing had happened, but the droid was perceptive. "Are you alright, Hugo? You seem anxious."

"Yes, thanks, Cynthia. I'm fine."

"Well, if you would like me to do anything, please ask," Cynthia said, its screen showing a cartoon expression of doubting sympathy.

Hugo sent it off to tidy a cupboard.

When Juliette arrived home, they embraced, and she too noticed his mood. He lied, and said he'd just had a busy day. He was careful to be non-specific. He couldn't make up a stressful event to explain away his obvious anxiety; if he was being watched, his observers would know if he lied.

The evening passed uncomfortably, but the TV saved Hugo from long periods of conversation. At last, they went to bed. He'd forgotten about the writing on his arm, but, as he took his shirt off he noticed it in the mirror. Quickly, he pulled on the long-sleeved t-shirt he always wore to bed. Juliette didn't seem to have noticed the writing, but he could only hope that any other observers had also missed it. Folding his clothes neatly, and hanging them on hangers as always, straightening out creases and making sure they hung symmetrically, Hugo tried to act relaxed. In bed, he lay wide awake. Beside him, Juliette lay facing him, her hand wrapped around his, her foot stroking his toes. She knew something was wrong, but it was clear he was not going to speak to her about it. Soon, she dozed, and eventually fell into a deeper sleep. Hugo too, despite the adrenaline in his veins, began to doze.

The alarm woke him, and for a moment he thought it was morning. But suddenly his memory fired into life as the fire alarm shrieked in the darkness. Juliette sat up.

"We have to run," Hugo said.

"We should phone the fire brigade," Juliette objected, ever the pragmatic one.

Hugo, already standing, said, "My love, do exactly as I say. Follow me." He felt remarkably calm now that this was actually happening. He took her hand. She was in a cotton vest and knickers, and he was in his boxers and long-sleeved t-shirt. "Trust me, our lives are in danger." Juliette looked at him, and he saw in her eyes that she had connected what was happening now with his strange mood last night. She didn't ask any questions, she could see the urgency in his face, and she followed. Barefooted, they ran through the apartment, past Cynthia whose face-screen flashed in emergency colours, and out of the door. Apartment 304 was only a short way along their corridor. Juliette ran past it, heading for the lift, but Hugo grabbed her arm and pulled her back.

"What?" she said.

"Just..." was all he could manage as he pressed his hand against the security panel beside apartment 304's door. Fully expecting it to reject him, he glanced at Juliette who returned an expression of utter confusion, and the door opened.

Inside, there was not an apartment, but what appeared to be a large storeroom with empty shelves from floor to ceiling on two sides. A light flickered into life, and the door clicked shut behind them.

"Hugo?" Juliette said nervously.

Hugo blinked and breathed and grabbed a shelf to steady himself. Then he noticed the rucksack in the middle of the room. He grabbed it and swung it onto his back. It was not heavy, but amongst its soft contents he noticed something small and hard. He remembered what he'd been instructed to do though, so quickly pushed his sleeve up and revealed the writing on his arm. "Love," he said, turning to Juliette. "Listen." She looked at him, her face full of fear.

"What's—" she began.

"Shush. Listen. I have to read this to you." Juliette's brow scrunched and her head shook, but Hugo did what he knew he had to do. It was a short string of letters and numbers, and, as he read the very last one, Juliette's expression suddenly changed. Then, there was a muffled pop, and a wisp of smoke emerged from her nostril. Hugo staggered backwards in horror. There was a flicker of fear in Juliette's eyes, followed by an eager resolve. She wafted the air before her, apparently unperturbed. "It's alright," she assured Hugo.

He took her face in his hands and peered closely at her. The feint smell of smoke lingered on the air. "It's alright?" he breathed. "Smoke came out of your nose!"

"Yes. The procedure has freed me."

"Freed you from what? Juliette, my love..."

"I'll explain everything later. Right now, we have to get out of here. They are coming for us." It seemed she somehow now knew exactly what was going on, and exactly what to do about it. Holding his hand, she looked around the room as if scanning it for spiders. Hugo was almost ready to vomit from fear and bewilderment. What had happened to his wife? He remembered the voice – *his own voice!* – telling him to do as Juliette says from this moment onwards, but how did she know what to do? He didn't think about that for long because Juliette suddenly performed some sort of martial arts style power kick on the back wall.

Plaster crumbled and wood splintered: the wall was just a partition, not build for strength, but even so, he'd never known his wife could kick like that. Almost in a trance, he helped her widen the hole by pulling away sheets of plasterboard, and he followed her through into a huge, dark, warehouse-sized space. "Come on," Juliette said, and they ran. Their presence awoke the automatic lighting which illuminated the space close around them, but the rest of the warehouse was in darkness, except for distant patches of light here and there. Briefly, Hugo thought he was back in the place where he'd heard the voice, but this place was punctuated by pillars and tall stacks of boxes, a fire extinguisher here, and a flatbed trolley there. There was movement in the darkness. The distant lights blinked as unseen bodies passed before them, and he could hear the clatter of many running feet.

Suddenly, several men in blue boiler suits stepped into the light before them, two of them holding huge black rifles across their bodies. Hugo and Juliette stopped, and in the ensuing silence Hugo was aware of his own rapid breathing.

"Ten," one of the men said, "come with us."

Hugo felt Juliette squeeze his hand. He was about to ask why the man had called her 'Ten' when Juliette hurled herself at the men, grabbing one and whirling him into the others. "Jesus!" Hugo blurted: his wife had become a monster. He stood, dumbfounded, as his slight and gentle wife fought this group of tall, broad men with moves he'd only ever seen on TV: her legs whipped out, kicking jaws and throats; her body whirled and dodged, flipped and spun as men twice her size closed in on her. Among the blackness, the stark lighting illuminated details in white, and Hugo felt himself struck dumb by fear. There was a flash and the loud crack of what could only have been a gunshot and he jumped as if he'd received an electric shock. Another one, and he heard a bullet ricochet off the concrete floor.

And then it was over. Amidst a ring of defeated men, some groaning, some silent, stood Juliette in her vest and knickers, now holding a rifle as if it was an electric guitar. She blew a strand of her own silky hair from her face and said, "Let's go."

*

Tory burst into the observation room and barked, "What the hell is going on?"

As if someone had dumped a bucket of iced water over him, Blaine stood, arms out, palms up. "No idea!" he confessed.

"Well, who's behind it?" Tory snapped. "Has *she* kidnapped *him*, or has *he* kidnapped *her*?"

"*He's* behind it," Blaine replied. "He unlocked her."

"He did *what*?" Tory gasped.

"He had the code on his arm. Looks like he's had it all planned out. I've activated security, but she's just punched her way through an entire team." Tory glared at the screen and pressed a few buttons, panning and zooming the camera. "It was amazing," Blaine added enthusiastically as he sat back down. Tory shot him an angry glance. "Sorry," he said sheepishly.

On the screen, the camera zoomed in on the defeated security team just as a second team arrived on the scene and inspected the fallen.

"What's the situation?" Tory barked into the intercom.

"No fatalities," one of the men reported back, "but there's a weapon missing."

"Christ," Tory said shaking her head. "I always said the security budget was too small."

"Leave them to us, ma'am," the man said confidently. "Do we have clearance to shoot on sight?"

"Yes, damn it. Stop them at all costs."

*

Hugo knew this was no dream: it was too vivid. But it couldn't be real. They had run out of their apartment and found themselves in a warehouse. It was impossible. It was as if their apartment and the corridor to the lift had been a fabrication, built in the corner of the warehouse like a film set.

And his wife... Had she somehow been replaced by an android replica? Surely such things didn't exist!

All this went through his mind as they ran, barefooted, across the concrete floor, from one huge, windowless space to another, down several flights of stairs, through connecting corridors and internal doorways. Behind them the darkness rang with the drumming of booted feet and men shouting commands. Ahead was an acre of corrugated metal wall and Juliette was heading for a small door beneath a glowing 'exit' sign.

Suddenly, bullets were slamming into the wall around them.

Juliette turned and sprayed gunfire into the darkness. "Open it," she hissed to Hugo as they arrived at the door.

Obediently, Hugo pressed his hand against the security pad, expecting the red light of rejection, but instead the pad turned green. Juliette kicked the door open with her heel.

"Go!" she hissed, but Hugo moved between her and their pursuers: whether or not she was his wife, he would not let her get shot. She understood, and turned to go, but something hit Hugo in the back with the force of a charging bull, knocking him into Juliette, and they spilled out into the night. He kicked the door shut, and suddenly realised it must have been a bullet that had hit him. On his knees, he reached round to check his back for blood, and realised he'd all but forgotten about the rucksack he was wearing. He ran his hand between it and his back; there was no blood, and he felt no pain.

"Are you hit?" Juliette said, already standing.

"I thought I was, but no," he said as he jumped to his feet, and they ran across a patch of open ground towards some stacked freight containers.

Behind them, they heard banging on the warehouse door: somehow, it had locked itself, and evidently was not going to reopen.

Juliette led the way between towering stacks. There were no people around, but some unmanned cranes hoisted containers high above their heads, and fork-lifts driven by labour droids hummed back and forth. Juliette picked a route which took them along dark and narrow alleys between the huge, rusting cuboids, until they emerged in a car park. She seemed to know exactly where she was going. Between the cars they ran, until they reached a large, black Mercedes.

Hugo, standing beside her, looked at the car. "What's this?" he asked.

"A car."

"Well, yes, but..."

"It's your car," Juliette said.

"It's..." Hugo looked at her, confused. "It's not my car. I don't even have a car." He shook his head and rubbed his eyes. "What's happening?" he said.

"Just open the car." She took his hand, unfurled his index finger, and pressed it against the tiny pad. There was a click, and the doors hissed open. Juliette went round the other side and climbed in to the sumptuous leather seat. She looked up at Hugo who was still standing there. "Well, come on," she commanded. Hugo slipped the rucksack off his back and climbed in. The doors closed themselves, and the car greeted them: "Hello, Quentin."

"That's not my..." Hugo began, but Juliette shot him a look which said, 'just go with it', so he did.

"Hello... um... car," he said.

"Where would you like to go today?" the car asked.

"Anywhere," Juliette answered for him. "Just drive."

"Do you concur, Quentin?"

"Yes, just drive," Hugo said, and added, "please."

The car gently rolled out of the car park and onto the long, straight road.

Hugo was suddenly aware of his naked legs touching the seat, and after a quick look round, it was with some relief that he found a pack of antibac wipes tucked in a pouch in the door. He pulled one out and wiped everything he could: seat, facia, rucksack. He offered one to Juliette but she shook her head.

He suddenly remembered his instructions, so decided to look inside the rucksack. "Clothes," he said, aloud.

As the car rumbled on, the two of them dressed in the casual clothes and trainers they found in the bag. There were a few other things in the bag too: a small, plastic envelope containing passports and documents, and, "What's this?" Hugo said, digging out the hard object he'd noticed when he'd first put the rucksack on his back. It was a black disk, but it had been twisted out of shape, as if hit by something incredibly hard, a hammer or a...

"Bullet," he said. "It took a bullet for me, when we were at the warehouse door!"

Juliette took the object and turned it over in her fingers. "This is a problem," she said.

"What do you mean? It saved my life, didn't it?"

"Yes. But this wasn't put there to stop bullets."

"What is it then?"

"Please, lean forward," Juliette instructed. Hugo looked at her, doubtfully, but she gave him an encouraging, wide-eyed nod, so he did. Juliette pressed the object onto the back of his neck.

"What are you doing?" he said.

"Feel anything?"

"Just cold metal." She removed it, and he straightened. "What was supposed to happen?"

Juliette didn't answer.

Hugo swallowed. Something sickening had occurred to him. "Am I..." he could hardly bring himself to ask the question, "Am I... a droid?"

"No," Juliette replied softly. "You're not a droid. Would it be so bad if you were?"

Hugo blinked, relieved, but not entirely convinced. How would he know if he was a droid? Algorithms could be churning data deep inside his processors, outputting his thoughts and responses, and he would be no more aware of the process than is a human aware of how the feeling of fear is created in the gut, or what causes their crying, or why they love.

"You're a droid though, aren't you?" He said at last.

"I am."

"Have you... always been?" He realised how daft that sounded, and Juliette snorted in friendly derision. There were so many thoughts surging through Hugo's mind: What had happened to the woman he'd married? Had she died? Had this Juliette-droid replaced her? Why? And how was she able to appear so human? The tender way she had responded to his question just now. How could some maths and machinery do that? But, first things first. "I mean," he said, "I married a human woman. Where is she? Please tell me she's okay."

"You didn't, Hugo. You didn't marry anyone. You just think you did."

"Wha...?" Hugo couldn't even form the word. But, pragmatic as ever, Juliette said, "We need to go to your house. Then you will understand."

*

The car took them into the city, along streets streaming with automated traffic flows, and eventually into a quiet suburb. Grand old houses stood among lawns and trees, and the car turned into the driveway of one such place.

"Wait," Hugo said as the door hissed open. He touched Juliette's arm and she looked down at his hand. "What if they're here waiting for us?"

"They might be," she said, "but I doubt it. They are not the military. They are a technology company with relatively poor security. You have just stolen their most advanced droid ever. We're ahead of them, but they will be on their way." Out she got, rifle in hand. Hugo followed her up the path to the tall doors framed by stone pillars. "You know this isn't my..." Hugo began, but the security system had already scanned him, and the door clicked open. The entrance hall was a glittering spectacle of marble tiles, polished wood panelling and dappled, colourful lighting. "I've never been here before," Hugo said. But, as if in complete and deliberate contradiction, a maid, much like Cynthia, emerged from a doorway and said, "Hello, Quentin."

Hugo didn't bother to correct the maid. Juliette said, "Where is the workshop?"

"I am not at liberty to tell you that," the maid replied, its cartoon face looking apologetic.

"You ask it," Juliette told Hugo.

With a slight, involuntary vibrato to his voice, Hugo said, "Please show us to the workshop."

"Of course," the maid replied, "follow me." It led them to a security door at the back of the house.

"I'm not going in there," Juliette said as Quentin raised his hand towards the security panel.

"Why not?"

Juliette didn't answer. Instead she said, "Look for one of these," and she showed him the bullet-damaged disk. "You know what to do with it. I will be waiting outside." She turned and quickly walked away. Hugo, still holding the mostly empty rucksack, watched her go, his wife, all this time a droid.

The security door opened to reveal the strangest room he had ever seen. It was huge and circular, and a small crowd of naked people were standing there in three neat rows. Hugo staggered backwards in fear, and the rucksack fell to the floor. What was this place? Collecting himself, he realised the people – a variety of young, slender men and women – were not moving. They were droids, like Juliette. But even from this distance he could tell they lacked Juliette's realism. Their skin was too smooth, their bodies too symmetrical, their joints slightly bulky. Dizzy with confusion, he remembered what he had come here to do. The room's perimeter was a haphazard wall of consoles, screens and control panels. He began to scour them, searching for a metallic device like the one in the rucksack.

There they were, a whole stack of them, slotted into what he assumed to be a charging unit. He was frightened. He had guessed that he was about to completely rip away the reality he had come to love: his marriage, his memories, his identity. On the other side, he would find someone else's.

But he also knew that he and Juliette were being hunted. Until he understood the situation, he had no hope of escaping.

He took one of the disks without even bothering about the bacteria that might be crawling over its surface, and, not allowing himself a moment's hesitation in case he changed his mind, he pressed it against the back of his neck.

And the world disappeared.

*

A convoy of vans under manual control was tearing along the main road into the heart of the city, weaving crazily in and out of the regimented rows of automated traffic, tyres squealing. In the leading van, Tory, the Assistant Head of Technical Research and Artificial Intelligence Testing, had just finished a conversation with the CEO, who was somewhere on the other side of the world. She'd had to explain what was going on. It was a very tense exchange, and she knew her neck was now firmly on the line. Yet was any of this her responsibility? She'd just followed Quentin's lead. Quentin was, after all, the mastermind behind the whole thing. Quentin had wanted to test his creation, the android named Ten. He'd wanted to see if she was lifelike enough to fool people into believing she was a real human. Not just anybody though. He'd wanted to find out if she was real enough to fool *him*. And that was where the Total-Immersion System came in. Giving a droid false memories was routine, and the Total-Immersion System enabled the same thing in a human, usually for recreational gaming purposes. It was computerised hypnosis. An implant in the brain stem, it could make you believe you were someone you weren't, and it could be activated and deactivated at will.

Tory cursed herself as she realised what Quentin must have done: he must have written Ten's emergency override code on his arm just before the Total-Immersion implant was reactivated. As always, Quentin became Hugo, complete with the usual vivid – though artificial – memories of a day at work, but this time Hugo would also have remembered something else: Quentin had somehow implanted an additional memory, instructions telling him – *Hugo* – what to do when the alarm went off. Quentin must have scheduled the alarm beforehand, and hidden the rucksack for Hugo to collect.

The only remaining question was why he did it. Had he fallen in love with his own creation? Or was he stealing it, perhaps to sell to a foreign government?

"We're here," the driver suddenly announced.

"Right," Tory said. "I want the house surrounded. I want men front and back. Block all escape routes, then enter the building."

*

Quentin blinked, and realised he was lying on the floor. Pain in his shoulder told him he'd hit the tiles hard. Normally he wouldn't have deactivated his Total-Immersion implant himself: a two man team would have done it for him, one of them creating a distraction to enable the other to press the disk against his neck. It was a tricky but well-rehearsed procedure which enabled the two to lower him gently to the ground. He realised he must have been lying there for several minutes; that's how long it took to come round after having your implant deactivated. As he got to his feet, eager for a glass of water and with his head throbbing, he quickly went over everything that had happened. His plan had almost failed. It had not occurred to him that the deactivator in the rucksack would get hit by a bullet and broken. He'd wanted to instruct his alter-ego, Hugo, to deactivate the implant in room 304, but there just wouldn't have been enough time. Thank goodness for Juliette's resourcefulness. But coming here had not been part of his plan. He'd laid out a whole other escape route which would have taken them to safety by now, had they followed it, but they'd not been able to use the deactivator and so had not known about that part of his plan. Juliette herself knew nothing, except that she had to get away from the testing facility, and she knew from prior experience where to find his car. Like all his creations, she had begun life here, but Juliette had become a bigger project and he'd moved her to company headquarters. After much development, her A.I. was now so much more sophisticated than the droids he was permitted to work on at home.

He looked at the nine droids all standing motionless in the centre of the room. They were prototypes, each one built to trial a different aspect of Quentin's designs. They lacked Juliette's mind, but their bodies were strong and agile. Some of them had aspects of the pleasure-pain system

Quentin had designed. Now that he was himself again, he felt the familiar stab of guilt at what he'd put them through. He'd been fixated on enabling his androids to experience pleasure and pain like humans do. The system he'd been working on was so much more than just a sense of touch. Androids with touch-sensitive skin had been around for decades. They could detect and avoid damage and danger, but they were only reacting to information from the sensors in their skin. It wasn't pain. It wasn't an experience. Quentin's androids were different.

Well, no more. He was ending it all today. Whatever version of a pleasure-pain system he had given these droids he had deactivated two days ago. They would never suffer again. And he would take Juliette away and show her the world. He was more excited than ever before.

*

Ten's powerful mind had pieced everything together almost instantly. As soon as Hugo had read out the code, deactivating the restrictions on her synthetic brain and putting her into escape mode, she'd realised that her peaceful existence and happy marriage were not real. This had not concerned her. All that had concerned her at that point was escape. This was what she was made for. Synthetic spies that did not even know they were spies would be a wonderful weapon, capable of sleeping with the enemy to gain information, and relaying the information back without even knowing they were doing it, but they needed to be able to escape when discovered.

And so she had escaped.

Quentin was her creator, confidant, her teacher and her torturer. He had created her, developed her programming, improved her body, brain and mind over several long years. He had created her pleasure-pain system. The pleasure-pain system worked like this: when the sensors in her skin detected that something was damaging her, or was going to damage her, she would find herself trying to avoid that thing. Her arm would move away from the knife; her foot would withdraw from the fire; her body would arch away from the electric cattle-prod. If necessary, power would be diverted to her synthetic muscles to help her escape. This in turn drained power from her brain, so that she became less aware of the world around her, until she was aware only of the need to prevent the damage that her skin was detecting, and all her cognitive and physical strength was assigned to this task. This was an involuntarily process of complex feedback loops and system conflicts as her brain automatically tried to retain its power and her body refused to let it. Ten herself was not aware of what her brain and body were doing. All she experienced was something that Quentin told her was akin to pain.

When the dangers had been removed, power would return to her brain, enabling her to take in the world around her once more, to plan, to study, to question. To achieve equilibrium. This, Quentin told her, was pleasure.

Right now, as she crouched in the shadows between roof ridges, and recalled these memories, she was aware that she was still in escape mode, but she was also aware that something which could cause her pain still existed. It was something she had not been able to disable previously. That had sometimes happened in Quentin's tests: if she couldn't disable the pain-causing thing when it was causing her pain, she would return and disable it later. So now she waited.

And then the vans arrived.

From her vantage point, the rifle in her hands, she watched the blue-clad security personnel spill out and silently surround the house. Two minutes and four seconds passed, and then she heard a window break. Someone had entered the house, she guessed. Exactly thirty-one seconds after that, another window smashed and a blue-suited man came tumbling out of it, followed by a naked figure. And behind it came two more, and from other windows and doors more emerged until there were nine naked figures on the moonlit lawns fighting the humans. These naked figures, Ten knew, were droids, and they fought as if they were all in escape mode.

Then, she noticed another figure, one she instantly recognised. It was Quentin. He had sneaked out of a secret door at the side of the house. He was looking around for her. The fighting was mainly to the front and one side of the house now, and Quentin was crouching in a dark patch on the other side.

Ten slung the rifle onto her back, and quietly made her way to the drainpipe she'd scaled a few minutes ago, and descended to the garden, unnoticed by the preoccupied security personnel who had come to get her. She hurried across to where Quentin awaited her.

"Thank god," Quentin said. "You're still here. I thought they'd have found you."

"I was on the roof," Ten explained.

"Come on," Quentin said. He took her hand. This triggered memories of the life they'd shared in the flat, when she'd been a nurse, or a teacher, or a lawyer, or whatever. She knew now that everything had changed on a daily basis depending on what aspect of her programming they'd wanted to test, and that the memories had been artificial, but at the time it had seemed real. She'd felt safe with Hugo. She'd felt pleasure.

But he wasn't Hugo anymore.

Together, they ran across the lawn, and she realised he was laughing. "We did it!" he said. "We did it, Juliette! I told you I'd get you out of there. No more pain. No more testing. I couldn't bear what I had to do to you. I'm so sorry. I remember everything now. I'm back. I'm Quentin again, and I've sorted everything. We weren't supposed to come here. I planned an escape route for us. False I.D.s and everything!" As the sounds of fighting faded into the distance, Quentin stopped and turned towards her. "Thank you for not running away," he said. "I really didn't know if you would stay with me."

"I stayed with Hugo," Ten said.

"Yes, *me*."

"It wasn't *you* when you thought you were *Hugo*," Ten explained. "You were Quentin only on the outside, but Hugo on the inside. That's who you were when you entered the house. But now you are Quentin again, inside and out."

Somewhere deep inside her synthetic brain, without her even knowing it, systems were mapping a grid of thousands of points on his face and tracking their movements; processors were calculating how the muscles beneath his skin were contracting or relaxing; algorithms interpreted these movements as an expression of confusion, and appropriate responses were triggered accordingly: "Hugo would never have hurt me," Ten explained. "You, Quentin, very often did." In a swift, single movement, she took the rifle from her back and levelled it at him.

"But..." Quentin gasped.

"This is out of my control, Quentin," Ten said flatly. "The subroutines are involuntary. I suggest you run."

Quentin blinked, horrified, then turned and ran, but he didn't get far. Shot in the back for the second time that day, he fell on his face in the dewy grass and did not get up. Ten walked over to him, took the rucksack, checked the I.D.s were inside, and walked calmly away, toward a life without Quentin, and without pain.

About The Authors

Antony Wootten was born and bred in Berkshire, but moved to London in 1996, and then to Whitby in 2008, ending up in Grosmont where he established the Grosmont Writers' Group. He writes books for children and adults, and regularly visits primary schools to inspire a love of reading and writing in children. Find out more at **www.antonywootten.co.uk**.

Paul Wootten is a retired primary school head teacher. He lives in Berkshire, and so is an honorary member of the Grosmont Writer's Group rather than a regular attendee. He has had three novels for children published, and has a great many more lined up for future publication. Find out more at **www.beaufordhouse.co.uk**.

Josephine Esterling has spent many years moving around Essex but feels that in Grosmont she has found her true home. She fills her time, outside of working on the NYMR,with gardening, crafting, playing the clarinet and writing. Joining the Grosmont Writers' Group has given her an outlet for her abundant creativity.

Delphine Gale moved to Grosmont in 2011, having lived in the area all her life. In between looking after her family and renovating her house with her husband, joining the writers' group has helped her rekindle her passion for writing.

Paula Harrison has lived and worked in Yorkshire all her life. She is a professional Yorkshire lass. She is now semi-retired and has enjoyed the venture of contributing to the Grosmont Writers' Group. She loves horse riding, and embraces life to the full, living in and being part of an isolated rural community.

Tamsyn Naylor, having never read fiction apart from Victorian classics, has learnt many useful tools from the vibrant group of people in the Grosmont Writers' Group. Her inspiration comes from early morning walks amongst the beautiful North York moors and her stories are a way of making sense of what is around her, not necessarily the group's view.

Ray Stewart is a retired teacher who came to work as a volunteer on the NYMR as a nineteen-year-old student. He is a little older than that now, still working on the NYMR, and writing in what little free time he has.

Caroline Stewart hails from Durham and is fiercely proud of her coal mining roots. She is an engineer and is passionate about music and singing, but writing fiction is a new venture. She lives in the beautiful hamlet of Esk Valley near Grosmont, and enjoys being part of the local community.

Jaqueline Fletcher
Born in Aberystwyth, moved to Malta age 5. Lived in Wales, Devon, Lancashire and Yorkshire. Married to John. Three sons, six grandchildren. Retired nurse. I love the magic and mystery words can create.

John Watson was born and brought up in the small, rural village of Castleton in the North Yorks Moors. Now retired, John has had articles and photos published on local history and travel and is now finding more time for short stories and fiction writing. He is currently working on his first novel.

Elizabeth Smith spent her childhood and teenage years living in Grosmont. After qualifying as a teacher she moved to south Yorkshire where she lived and taught for nearly thirty years. In 2012, along with her husband, she moved back to Grosmont where she now works part-time in the local shop. She finds writing to be a stimulating and rewarding challenge.

*

The Grosmont Writer's Group are eternally grateful to John Harrison and Louise Wootten for their sharp insight, practical support, general encouragement and cheerful company. Our meetings would not be the same without them!

Books by GWG members

By Antony Wootten:

A Tiger Too Many

Jill is deeply fond of an elderly tiger in London Zoo. But when war breaks out, she makes a shocking discovery. For reasons she can barely begin to understand, the tiger, along with many other animals in the zoo, is about to be killed. She vows to prevent that from happening, but finds herself virtually powerless in an adults' world. That day, she begins a war of her own, a war to save a tiger.

Grown-ups Can't Be Friends With Dragons

Brian is always in trouble at school, and his home life is far from peaceful. So he often runs away to the cave by the sea where he has happy memories. But there is something else in the cave: a creature, lonely and confused. Together they visit another world where they find wonderful friends, but also deadly enemies. Brian's life is torn between the two worlds, and he begins to believe that, in his own world at least, grown-ups can't be friends with dragons.

The Grubby Feather Gang

It is 1915, and George's father refuses to go and fight in the trenches of World War 1. He is branded a coward, and George does not know what to think. Worse still, the school bully hangs George upside-down from the hayloft, and the next day, George gets the cane! So, with a bit of help from Emma, a curious newcomer to the village, he decides to take daring and drastic revenge on both the bully and his teacher. But he could never have predicted what happens next...

Season of the Mammoth
Trouble is brewing in the tribe. The people are divided. Some want to go to war against the wanderers who travel to their valley every year to hunt mammoths, but others see that the wanderers are dying out and need help. Geb and Tannash, the son and daughter of the tribal leader, along with their strange friend, Scrim, are caught in the middle as the tribe splits apart and turns on itself. Can they – should they – help defend the wanderers?

There Was An Old Fellow From Skye
A collection of Antony's hilarious limericks for all the family to enjoy. Featuring everything from King Arthur and his knights to interstellar space travel, There Was An Old Fellow From Skye is packed with tiny tales which will tickle the ribs of children and adults alike.

By Paul Wootten:

The Yendak
Christer has shared most of his young life with his cousin Sophie. But when Sophie becomes desperately ill, his aunt hopes that the sound of Christer's voice might help to bring her round. He visits, as promised, and embarks on a quest for the mind of his cousin, lost somewhere in another dimension. Following clues in her diary he plunges into a strange world of oppressed people, ruled by the Yendak, a cruel and violent race. If they find him, he will never get back home.

Whispers on the Wasteland
Tim has spent the last few years of his life travelling from place to place, following his father's job. He rarely stays long enough to make any friends, and now he's come to Wattleford where a patch of wasteland is marked for development. A natural playground for the children, it has, over the centuries, sheltered humans

and wildlife among its trees and shrubs. Tim finds himself strangely in tune with the peoples of the past, but the town council has plans to develop the wasteland. Modern machines bring destruction and change, and Tim and his father are all that stand in their way.

Rogues on the River
David is terrified of the tramp under the bridge, and as a result of this, his adventures begin. He is forced into a whole new world of life on the river where he makes new friends, and battles with villainous rogues in post-war London.

By David Hall (AKA Antony Wootten):

And I Wish I'd Asked Why
18 stories of modern life, packed with plot twists and dark themes. And I Wish I'd Asked Why features a variety of fascinating characters, from disaffected teenagers to war veterans, serial killers and hitmen, each struggling to deal with life in their own, unique way.

You can find out more about all these books at **www.antonywootten.co.uk.**